PRINTED IN BEIRUT

Karam Brothers 8 Est. 1908

a novel by Jabbour Douaihy
translated by Paula Haydar

Interlink Books

An imprint of Interlink Publishing Group, Inc.
Northampton, Massachusetts

First published in 2018 by

Interlink Books
An imprint of Interlink Publishing Group, Inc.
46 Crosby Street, Northampton, MA 01060
www.interlinkbooks.com

Library of Congress Cataloging-in-Publication Data
Names: Duwayhåi, Jabbåur author. | Haydar, Paula, translator.
Title: Printed in Beirut / Jabbour Douaihy ; translated from the Arabic by Paula
   Haydar.
Other titles: òTibi°a fåi Bayråut. English
Description: First American edition. | Northampton, MA : Interlink Books, 2018.
Identifiers: LCCN 2018028224 | ISBN 9781623719906
Subjects: LCSH: Publishers and publishing--Lebanon--Beirut--Fiction. | Money
   laundering—Lebanon—Beirut—Fiction. | GSAFD: Suspense fiction.
Classification: LCC PJ7820.U92 T5313 2018 | DDC 892.7/37—dc23
LC record available at https://lccn.loc.gov/2018028224

Printed in the United States of America

To request our complete 48-page catalog, please call us
toll free at 1-800-238-LINK, visit our website at
www.interlinkbooks.com, or write to
Interlink Publishing, 46 Crosby Street, Northampton, MA 01060

for Fares Sassine

1

In the middle of a sweltering summer oppressing the city of Beirut during the second decade of the twenty-first century, a young man with high arched eyebrows, evidently stuck that way from always saying no, was getting off a city bus with ads on both sides that read, "Never forget those kidnapped, held captive, or disabled by war." He was holding a thick red notebook tight to his chest, over his heart, looking like someone with his arm in a sling because it was broken or had a bullet-wound. He marches forward, briskly clicking the heels of his new shoes against the pavement, and storms past the wilting trees and the slow-moving pedestrians—inconvenient obstructions in the way of very important business.

He enters a building with a dark basalt stone relief adorning its entrance that was hit at one time by gunfire, causing the stone relief to become doubly abstract. He adjusts his bright red necktie in the elevator mirror before going in to see a man of indeterminate age with a poster for *The Three-Penny Opera*, in German, adorning his office wall. This man, wearing his thick glasses, had been sitting at his desk all morning, outsmarting his boredom by putting that legendary memory of his, proverbial among his friends, to the test: typing, from memory and with only one finger, the entire *Mu'allaqa*[1] of Zuhayr Bin Abi Sulma. He included every diacritical mark, and for each verse he chose a different font, running the entire gambit of all available Windows fonts. He was in the midst of typing, in Andalus Medium, with his right index finger up in the air, the famous line:

War is naught but what you have lived and suffered
And what people say about war is not a story written in the stars

when this tall young man suddenly appeared before him and introduced himself.

"Good day. I am Farid Abu Shaar."

"Abu *Shaar*? Mr. *Hair*? Is that a pen name?"

The young man doesn't appreciate the joke from the publisher who now has his notebook and is giving it a careful looking over. He opens to the first page and whistles in surprise, raising his eyebrows as he reads out loud, *The Book to Come*.

"That's the title of a book by Maurice Blanchot," he adds in clear frustration, and then returns the notebook to the young man, telling him they stopped accepting handwritten manuscripts ten years ago, at least, and that they also quit publishing poetry collections. They were taking up so much space in the warehouse, they started giving them away free to anyone who wanted one. The young man protests, saying his book is not poetry, but the man sitting behind his desk quickly gives his definitive answer on the matter.

"We quit publishing prose, too!"

Farid Abu Shaar clenches his right fist and goes on his way. The sharp comeback he did not give to the rude fatso typing the *Muʿallaqa* of Zuhayr on his computer gets mumbled instead into the backseat of the taxi taking him to his home in the nearby Furn al-Shubbak suburb. He gets home, and his mother immediately starts complaining about her aches and pains, and the varicose veins that only started appearing on her legs after giving birth to him, the youngest of three boys. "You were a big baby. Five kilos."

She feeds him tripe, having taken care to clean it with lemon juice and stuff it generously with onions and pine nuts, the way he likes it. Afterward, he takes a nice nap on the sofa in front of the TV.

2

The next day, he has an appointment near the remodeled but still defunct Beirut Port lighthouse. Its fresh black-and-white paint glimmers in the morning sunlight. His meeting is with a woman smoking a long, thin cigar who orders him a coffee without asking. She leafs through the pages of his notebook with her index finger and examines it. She has a photograph of her father there in front of her on her desk. His thick hair is slicked back and he's leaning against the stone column at the entrance to the Sorbonne, accompanied by Maxime Rodinson. He left the publishing house to his daughter, who now puffs lightly on her cigar while adding numbers on a yellow notepad. She raises her head and discovers her client silently waiting and watching her. Confident, brunette, attractive—the quintessential tough Beiruti woman. She cuts right to the chase.

"Four thousand U.S. dollars, and you can have two hundred complimentary copies."

He cringes with displeasure, and she adds, "Printing and typesetting and editing…"

He tries to object, but she silences him by standing up, taking him by the hand, and showing him to the door. "No one reads," she says in a conciliatory tone. "Either we close our shop doors, or behave like ladies of the night…"

He walks on, dejected, and consoles himself that the person who takes the time to read his book carefully will have something very different to say.

He climbs the stairs to the fifth floor, the sweat from his palms embossing dark splotches on the cover of his red notebook. In his Armenian accent, Avedis, the owner of Dar al-Rawa'i Publishing House, apologizes that he only specializes in publishing "ancient" texts—*The Perfumed Garden of Sensual Delight*, *Tuhfat al-Arous* (The Bride's Boon)—and works claiming to be original, erotic editions of *The Thousand and One Nights*. Books purchased primarily by women, so he says. And so, Farid Abu Shaar goes on his way, without smiling in response to Avedis's wink about that last comment.

At the coffee shop, he meets a publisher who works out of his car. He comes in in a hurry, wearing his black glasses, and opens the laptop on the table in front of him. When he says he specializes exclusively in electronic publications, Farid apologizes, saying his heart was set on a book made of paper. So, the publisher goes on his way, leaving not a trace—except the scent of a man's cologne clinging to the perspiration in the atmosphere and dissipating in an aroma of wild pine.

In his air-conditioned office, Subhi al-Ja'bary takes the notebook from Farid, places it in front of him, clasps his hands over it, and begins narrating an anecdote he's in the process of composing as an introduction to the autobiography he wants to write—an idea that has been gelling in his mind for some time. After taking part in a protest march in Aleppo against secession from Egypt, he was sentenced to death. So to escape the secret service he disguised himself as a woman and fled to Beirut.

"They followed me here and shot at me on Hamra Street with the intent to kill me, but despite that I lived how I liked. I adored women, smoked Cuban cigars, drank whiskey, and published a magazine in which I said whatever I wanted to say."

What he doesn't mention is that he also translated Marquez and pirated books by Naguib Mahfouz without paying copyright fees.

He escorts Farid to the elevator and says good-bye without ever having opened his notebook.

The only one to sympathize with him is Salim Khayyat, because Farid reminds him of his wife. Every piece of writing reminds him of her. She wrote poetry, even from the mountain sanatorium where she vied with the illness that eventually destroyed her. He established the publishing house for her sake, to publish her poetry collections and her friends' writings. The only reason he was putting in hours at the press now was to catch a whiff of her in that place. He gives Farid a copy of her last book, *Archives of the Heart*, a collection of scattered papers from her desk drawer.

On his way down the stairs, Abu Shaar flips open to a random page and reads.

> *Beirut, the rose-colored city*
> *Where thoughts and caravans are emptied out—*
> *The final sanctuary of the East*
> *Where the son of man receives a cloak of light…*

A dazzling wave crashes over his chest, and he fears being defeated by the tender, deceased poetess. So, he shuts her book and looks for a trash can to rid himself of that poetry collection. With the sun setting between the minarets of the Grand Blue Mosque, he makes one last stop at "Karam Brothers Press, Est. 1908." He walks uphill on a narrow road that leads him through an oasis of lilac trees, as if he's left the city. He sees two cats playing in the courtyard, and he can smell ink. He is greeted by a man with a scar on his cheek—a deep wound that had obviously been stitched up. Abdallah—or "Dudul"—the current owner and inheritor of the press. He listens to Farid, inspecting his attire.

When Farid says he's hoping to publish the book, an answer comes from inside, from the back corner of the room, in broken Arabic. "What's in the book?"

He hadn't noticed her there when he first came in. She was sitting on a leather chair reading *To Kill a Mockingbird*, in French.

"I squeezed the juice of my being into this book!"

Abdallah translates what Farid said into French for his wife who, in an involuntary motion, had reached over with her right hand to the manuscript as if this "juice" he mentioned would be clear to her the moment she flipped to the first page.

"We have an opening for an Arabic language copyeditor…"

The press owner's suggestion bewilders Farid. He can feel the woman's eyes on his back. He asks for some time to think it over, which Abdallah hopes won't be long.

۞

He comes back at the start of the next week with his notebook in hand. The two cats are still there. This time the man is all alone in his office, with no trace of the woman. He notices a small icon of the Virgin Mary, "Mistress of the Seas," stuck to the massive new digital printing press. They show him to the copyeditor's desk, which is in the middle of a vast hallway jam-packed with equipment and desks and workers. He tells himself he will never get used to the smell of ink, but in the end, he does.

2

He also got used to that frowning face in the black-and-white picture hanging inside its gilded frame on the stone column in the middle of the hall. Fuad Karam, the printing press's "founding father."

Fuad had been in the middle of his third decade of life when the summer of 1914 came, and along with it the news of war breaking out in every direction. He and his older brother agreed that one of them should leave Beirut, so that they wouldn't both be in the same place when the situation heated up. One of the two brothers would travel, completing the journey their father had begun when he set out from Aleppo, stopped in Lebanon on his way to the land of the Nile, and fell in love with their mother. She was his cousin, the daughter of his maternal uncle who had hosted him in Lebanon. He ended up staying in Beirut, satisfied with a simple life.

Who would go and who would stay was a decision the brothers agreed to leave up to chance.. They went together to Souk Ayyas: If they were approached by a beggar asking for alms, then the older brother would get to choose; but if they met up with the newspaper vendor, then it would be up to Fuad. As soon as they reached the fountain, a shabbily dressed young man with a disturbed look about him pounced on them. They thought he was a poor beggar looking for a handout, until he slipped a copy of *Al-Qustas* (The Scales of Justice) newspaper inside Fuad's jacket. The paper had been banned from print by Bakir Sami Basha, the Wali of Beirut. Then the man disappeared down an alley, just as he had appeared, without asking for anything in return. The brothers read the headline: The French Protectorate and Annexation of Beirut with Mount Lebanon. They vied with each other to tear up the newspaper and throw it away, looking around fearfully as they did so, worried there might be an informant lurking nearby. They considered the young man to be a newspaper vendor, and called Fuad the winner. Still not having settled on an opinion, he got tongue-tied at first, before suddenly hearing himself spit out, "I'll stay in Beirut!"

After handing over the key to his house, his brother bid him farewell, boarded the Italian ship *Syracusa*, and headed to Alexandria with his inconsolable wife who cried uncontrollably as she said good-bye to her parents and family. She continued to wave her white handkerchief at them even after they'd gone back home and the city had disappeared from her view into the distant horizon.

The war was quick to fulfill its promise, and the day the crew of the German frigate Goyim announced their nation was joining in, they all exploded with joy. They lifted Admiral Souchon, who they called "the Seafox," up on their shoulders and jubilantly paraded him on deck, leaving big grease stains on his crisp white uniform. They belted out their war anthems as they sailed to Istanbul. They participated in the bombing of Odessa and Sevastopol, and snickered at the sound of their Turkish allied officers exchanging commands atop the decks of the Hamidian frigate. In their turn, the Ottomans also declared a general call to arms, mobilizing three million conscripts inside the Sultanate, three hundred thousand of whom would die in battle while another half million would succumb to disease, malnutrition, lack of supplies, and shabby clothing. The British blocked off the sea, and rumors made their way to Beirut. The Maronite inhabitants picked up whatever was "light in weight" and "heavy in value," and fled on horse buggies that happened to be making their way back to their mountain villages. Throngs of Muslims crammed onto the train to Damascus, and the Druze made their way by land to their relatives in Hauran. All the black coal was depleted, and all the mulberry trees in the nearby mountains were chopped down to keep the trains moving. The world was bursting at the seams with commoners while Turkish officers drank champagne in rich people's houses and played bridge surrounded by beautiful women and violinists.

Fuad Karam, who was still known as Fuad Karroum at the time, said to himself that his older brother always had the better luck. He spent anxious nights worrying about not having enough food in the house. Around midnight, as he gazed at his sleeping wife, a persistent thought nagged at him. He should leave everything behind and travel secretly to Haifa, then on to Arish, and from there to Cairo—to start a new life, instead of this difficult one he'd begun in Beirut. But then he snaps out of his delirium, remembering that his wife sleeping there beside him is pregnant and he would never leave her. He gets up and goes to the window, calculating his savings for the thousandth time. He doesn't go back to sleep until one of the novice monks at Saint Joseph's Church inside the Jesuit monastery across the street rings the bell for the first matins prayers.

Jamal Basha arrived in the town of Alay, wearing his military uniform and tall fur cap. The people of the town greeted him with tens of meters of red carpet, and he delivered a speech to them, saying, "The Ottoman Empire is your mother. She has compassion for you and protects you from foreigners. Obey her laws so you may live in peace." He returned to Beirut the next year, accompanied by Anwar Basha, the Minister of War, and with the defeat that Major General Sir John Maxwell inflicted

9

upon him in the Suez Canal—where he'd tried to carry out a military assault with five thousand camels (not including mules)—weighing heavily on his frowning face. The crowds of beggars descending from the mountains were shooed away so that the eyes of the two leaders of the Association of Union and Progress would not fall upon them. With the list of death-sentenced criminals in his pocket, Jamal arrived at a dinner invitation he had accepted from the jeweler Yusuf al-Hani. One of his officers came and whispered to him out on the balcony that his host was one of the signatories of the petition seeking foreign protection, which had been discovered hours earlier on the walls of the French Consulate. The commander left the dinner party with a pallid face, after shaking hands with al-Hani and his wife, and sentenced him to be hanged a few days later.

For days, Fuad Karam dreaded falling asleep at night, for fear of being haunted by a dream in which he saw himself trying in vain to catch a strange bird that kept getting away from him. When he opened his hands, he would see them covered in blood. One night, he heard shouts coming from the monastery. Orders given in Turkish and Arabic, and responses in French and Italian. Then the sound of a door slamming, and a threat, followed by silence interrupted only by the pattering of soldiers' boots on the monastery's floor tiles. In the morning, Father Lambert, the Belgian priest with the bent back Fuad always saw sitting reading on the church steps, told him that they were going to choose an American monk, whose country had not entered the war, Father McCourt, to keep guard over the possessions of the Jesuits, who had been warned they must leave the country. Around noon, people came out onto the rooftops. The children cheered while the adults tried to restrain them and looked out to the horizon, waiting for a warship of unknown nationality that would bombard Beirut at sundown, it was rumored. People talked about running out of flour before it actually did run out, and about hunger before famine felled its first victims. Hunting was prohibited and there began to appear on the streets of Beirut throngs of beggars who came from their starving villages carrying nothing but their emaciated bodies.

The Jesuits distributed the gold chalices, as well as the scientific scales and surgical tools from the medical school, and all the carpets, the monks' robes, and the prayer books, to some trustworthy neighboring Christian families who came regularly to Holy Mass at Saint Joseph's Church. Then some three hundred monks and nuns—Mariamites, Lazarites, Capuchins, Franciscans, and others hailing from Palestine and Syria, all climbed aboard a boat equipped to carry fifty passengers and set off for the Greek shores. No sooner did they leave the port of Beirut than they all began chanting in Latin the Hail Mary prayer, beseeching her to save them from imminent drowning.

At the very same time, Fuad was running into the mule cart driver who went around picking up whatever poor soul happened to have died from hunger or illness on the side of the road. He would throw a cloth over him and cart him slowly to the Bashoura Cemetery. Fuad used to see him in the afternoons. One time he happened upon him on a narrow lane. When the man smiled at him, Fuad turned his face away and picked up his pace, hurrying to get away from the man singing a Baghdadi *mawwal*[2] to himself with the corpse stretched out on the cart behind him. But this time he saw him at night, just before falling off to sleep. He caught a glimpse of him through his window. The man was stopped in front of the gate to the monastery, accompanied by a tall man wearing a tarbush. Not long after, a troop of soldiers followed behind them. Ghosts in the light of the moon advancing on the Jesuit monastery. After checking to make sure his wife was asleep, Fuad went out, closed the door behind him, and followed after them across the street. If they stopped him, he would claim that the monks had put him in charge of guarding the monastery before they left. They lit a lantern and entered the rear building. Fuad stayed close to the stone wall, listening.

"You want this paper cutter, the lithograph press, and all the sewing, gilding, and book binding equipment?"

"Everything. Everything."

"The big double press machine cannot be transported just like that. It's impossible to carry it. It must be taken apart. You work here, and you know it well, Halwany. You can take it apart here now, and then go to Damascus and reassemble it there. And don't forget all the typefaces. The Wali insisted on ten languages. Arabic, French, Latin, Armenian, and others. And the books. All the books…"

He hesitated a little before adding resolutely, "You'll move everything in two or three trips to the train station in Karantina. Everyone will meet here, at this same time. We'll finish up before dawn and be on our way."

Fuad heard enough and then slipped away unnoticed. They came back five days later. Big carriages and an army of porters accompanied by an entire troop of soldiers. They came at night but found nothing to transport. The place had been cleaned out. So, they turned around and went back to inform the Wali.

The next day, the Turkish officers were caught up in the tense news surrounding the impending arrival of French frigates to the Lebanese shores and the nearing of the time for their withdrawal from Beirut and other countries their forefathers had conquered in 1516. The hearse driver kept the money that was supposed to go to the porters and carriage owners who had come to move the printing press, and no one came back to ask about it.

3

"Karam Brothers Press, Est. 1908"

Fuad changed the spelling of his family name from Karroum to Karam, in 1922, the year the French conducted the first census, which the Muslims boycotted. Just like that, with the stroke of a pen, the son of a grain retailer from Aleppo became a Lebanese citizen registered in the Medawar neighborhood of Beirut, without ever having lived there a single day. He claimed to be a Maronite, because he felt that the Syriac Catholic sect his family belonged to, the language of which his father spoke fluently, was a tiny minority that would have little influence in the new State of Greater Lebanon. And so, the registrar recorded him as a Maronite, based on an affidavit signed by one of the district mayors of Beirut. Likewise, Fuad linked himself and his descendants to a popular family, the Karams, who were scattered throughout the Levant and were represented among its various religious sects. The Karams were so numerous it was difficult to ascertain how they were all related to each other.

A hundred years began in the vicinity of the old Russian Consulate in Beirut, where in the beginning Fuad worked the press himself during the day, along with his partner, Abdelhamid al-Halwany, and then at night, he put whatever profits he was able to scrape together toward opening bottles of champagne for the young Greek girls. They tried to teach him to dance the Hasapikos and laughed at him for being so fat. They snickered behind his back when he traded in his tarbush for a European hat. The moment he appeared in the doorway at the entrance to the cabaret, they raced each other to greet him. He headed home very late, after drinking so much he wound up in a dark alley, where he was greeted by a mugger's blow to the head and ended up flat on his back and unconscious until dawn. When they discovered him, his jacket had been stolen, along with the gold pound he kept in his pocket for emergencies. He squandered his income, and his wife threatened to do things to him that she could not possibly do. But luck was on his side. The schools reopened and the papers and journals came back into print after the war. If *Al-Nibras* magazine went out of print, then *The New Woman* took its place. And after *Al-Maʿaref* journal came *Al-Fawaʾid*. His revenues doubled, he hired new employees, and when the place became too cramped, he moved southeast to a huge ground floor space on the Damascus highway.

There he started printing calendars illustrated with icons of the saints, calling cards, and stationery for use by the French Mandate forces. While the employees worked on setting the type or cutting the paper, they would watch out the window as the dead were buried over at the Melkite Greek Catholic Church cemetery. They grew accustomed to seeing the pretty, fair-skinned early morning visitor wandering through the marble crosses and angel statues with a bouquet of daisies in her arms. It was there at the new location that Fuad arrived one morning with difficulty, out of breath, on a day in which a downpour of epic proportion drowned Beirut, causing Fuad to be concerned about the press. His fears came true when he got there and found all the machines and the paper supply immersed under a flood of water. His face grew dark, and when he saw the precious copy of the Quran, the one with the ornate diacritics that was printed on rare paper, and the book, *The Essence of Molten Gold in the Condensed Biographies of Kings*, both immersed in a pool of water with their ink starting to run and bleed, he couldn't breathe. He went out to the street, to the open air, in the pouring rain, and collapsed onto the ground. After a few days in the nearby Hôtel Dieu de France Hospital, he died.

⚜

His son moved the press north, out of grief at the loss of his father and also out of fear of another flood, to a street that had recently been named after Abd al-Wahhab al-Engleezi, who the Turks hanged in Damascus and was counted among the heroic martyrs who died for Lebanese independence. He added weekly lottery tickets and horse racing bulletins to his printing repertoire and suffered through complaints from residents of the building and in the neighborhood on account of all the noise from the machinery that sometimes ran day and night. It woke them up in the morning and prevented them from napping in the afternoon. Women would come out on their balconies and curse the workers as they left the press at the end of their shift. Policemen would step in on their behalf and come back with their pockets filled with bribes from the Karam family that would keep them quiet for months. Then the neighbors' household garbage would find its way onto piles blocking the press's entrance or get thrown through a window left open at night. Defamatory remarks and complaints came from every direction, with people claiming there were sick people who could not bear all the noise, until the son of Fuad Karam finally chose to flee from that little civil war. At any rate, he'd outgrown the location once again after importing a new model offset printing machine. He was also able to penetrate Beiruti social circles when he married into one of the first families to bring American cars onto the local market and the first to raise and train Arabian racehorses in Beirut.

Karam Brothers Printing Press spent more than two decades in its location near Sagesse High School. The press contracted all the school's publications, textbook series, report cards, and the renowned literary magazine that carried the school's name. The city was flourishing, and business was booming, muddied only by a rift between the two grandsons of Fuad Karam, which was unavoidable after their father's early death. Two young brothers who failed to transform the family business into a commercial institution run by one fundamental rule: what's yours is yours and what's mine is mine. When some lawyer friends of theirs advised them to form a Limited Liability Company and two representatives from Beirut Maronites and Christian Minorities intervened to settle their dispute, the chasm between them only widened after a public exchange of accusations against each other. The younger brother accused the older brother, Lutfi Karam, of being greedy and manipulative and prayed to God not to satisfy his greed. And the older brother cast doubt on the younger brother's abilities after he'd made a number of terrible and costly mistakes. The whole thing was helped along by their wives, a result of the various manifestations of jealous animosity that existed between them.

Eventually, the younger brother left the press. He cried in exasperation and sold his share for a large sum of money as a way to compensate himself for the pain of separation he was suffering that made him go so far as to hire a lawyer to have his family name changed. His brother borrowed the required amount of money to buy his brother out, and the younger brother was forced to sell his share of his mother's house and of some shops in Souk Nouriyyeh they had inherited from her. He attended his mother's funeral like a stranger, didn't have dinner with his brother's family who had taken care of their old mother in her final days, and took off as soon as the line of guests offering condolences started to break up. His wife sent a wreath of flowers along with an apology for not being able to attend because her due date was imminent. The following day, one day after her mother-in-law passed away, she gave birth to a baby girl. The cast out brother tried to start his own printing press to prove his superiority, but his father-in-law persuaded him to work with him in the steel industry where he raked in big profits and still continues to do so.

ᵔᘔᕊ

Lutfi ran the press by himself and encouraged his son Abdallah to major in business administration. He also rented a large warehouse in the Gemmayze district to the northwest where, thanks to his cleverness and knowledge, he was able to coexist with the various militias during the war. When the value of the Lebanese lira plummeted, all the bank debts he'd incurred from his falling out with his brother shrank to paltry sums he was able to pay off easily. One of his final decisions was to move the press west, into the house he inherited from his mother, and turn over ownership to his son Abdallah—"Dudul"—who married a young woman who Lutfi would have preferred to be a bit less beautiful if he had been asked. Lutfi continued to frequent the place—he and his walking stick and great cunning—because, apart from a few hours he spent in the afternoons playing cards at the Aeroclub, his days were empty.

That was how, with an unseen will from above, as though the hand of an inscrutable architect was guiding a giant compass, Karam Brothers Printing Press traced out a full circle, with radii that were nearly equal in length, around a central point: The Church of St. Joseph, Patron Saint of Jesuit fathers. This all happened during those decades when Beirut was bombed from the sea by warships and from the mountains by cannons, was besieged and defiled by armies, airstrikes, and uprisings that had lost sight of their objectives, and when barricades got set up for opposing sides to fight behind. It was a time when Beirut tasted life's swagger and its magnificence, the idleness of days overlooking the sea, and the clamor of nights that concealed the poor, the famous, the dancers, and the spies. The Press traced out its circle, finally settling under those high arched ceilings surrounded by the jacaranda trees with their purple flowers, that place to where Farid Halim Abu Shaar came, in the heat of his failing attempts to publish his book, at a time when his lack of employment and dire need for income, combined with some flirtatious glances from a woman's clear blue eyes, were enough to make him settle down in that place as its unparalleled Arabic language copyeditor.

4

Farid worked hard at his new job. He wasn't friendly with his coworkers, preferring to talk to himself rather than suffer their chitchat and fake comradery. He kept busy until leaving the press at day's end and had no idea that those arched cellars he worked in had been spacious enough in their heyday to house ten purebred Arabian horses of the highest pedigree. Those cellars also provided lodging for two trainers and a stableman who, dressed in their special clothes, would trot the horses out on Sundays for a showy parade around the area after their return from the racetrack. It was said that the jacaranda trees—ten seedlings in soil that Lutfi's mother brought back with her on the ship from Buenos Aires that grew into large, mature trees there—were so fragrant during blossom season that they invigorated the horses, giving them extra speed that was apparent in every race of the season.

Above the arched cellars, another expansive story was built for living quarters. It had a high ceiling and a separate main entrance with a wrought iron door that led to an open area where a white marble statue of Venus stood with her naked behind. Parts of the statue were covered by a climbing vine of fragrant native jasmine. Lutfi Karam's mother inherited the house and her brother inherited the valuable horses, which he transported to a farm in the Beqaa Valley. The floors of the arched cellars were paved with granite tiles and the walls were sandblasted and power washed to remove the moss and herbage, revealing and giving prominence to the keystone, and transforming the place into an open hall for the printing press, which was around thirty meters long. Two partition walls were put in to section off administrative offices, one of which was run by Abdallah Karam, who also sectioned off a cellar in the back to preserve the business's history. There he kept the original printing machines, the boxes of typeface blocks that used to be set by hand, and the rare books that were salvaged from the flood that inundated the press on the Damascus highway.

The living quarters were connected to the hall below by means of a narrow stone stairway inside the building that led whoever was climbing up the stairs directly and unexpectedly into the kitchen, right between the refrigerator and the marble sink. People downstairs sitting at their computers or engrossed in their page layout work could ascertain who might be coming down the stairs starting with their feet. The proprietor, Abdallah, who came at precisely 8:30 in the morning, could be identified by his quiet, thick crepe rubber soles and his heavy footsteps in the direction of his office, especially after the big accident that almost took his life. His wife, when she infrequently appeared at the press, was known by her high heels and perfectly shaped white legs, at least when she wasn't wearing long pants. And one could tell it was cheerful Fleur, who was always flitting about, by the sudden rush down the stairs that cost her on one occasion to trip and tumble all the way to the bottom, her head covered in blood.

Fleur, the Karam family's maid from the "Island of a Hundred Windmills" in Guadalupe, got together with some fellow countrywomen in the courtyard of Our Lady of the Assumption Church after Sunday mass. In fluent French they would exchange news about their distant archipelago and share anecdotes about the Beiruti families they served. Fleur liked to say that she was content. She helped her "mistress" dress her twin daughters and walked them to the school bus stop in the morning. She would come back to the house and find her sitting at the window smoking and talking on her cell phone, either holding back her laughter or whispering in secrecy. Fleur was eager to say more. She wanted to tell her girlfriends that she'd been awakened at night by the sound of movement in the house—"Madame" pacing back and forth in the living room, exhaling loudly. One time she heard her open the kitchen door and go downstairs to the press, but she got tired while waiting for her to return and fell back to sleep. Fleur looked into the eyes of her countrywomen wondering if they could be trusted with Persephone's secrets. She remembered the lady of the house's kindness and the extra money she gave her, whether there was an occasion for it or not, and at the last second decided not to divulge her secret.

Persephone Melki, or "Perso" to her friends, earned a degree in Interior Design from the Lebanese Academy of Fine Arts. She married Abdallah soon after graduating and before having a chance to practice her profession. Her marital home above the press, which was inaugurated with a memorable celebration, was her first artistic achievement and a project she completed in preparation for their marriage. *Al-Buyut wa al-A'mal* magazine did a four-page illustrated exclusive about how Persephone Melki painted the gypsum of the ceiling and the walls with gradations of pink, colors whose green tint she mixed by hand, and then augmented, with utmost patience and skill, with a layer of transparent wax that allowed for the walls to be washed with water. She placed deep mirrors in engraved frames at the entryway and in the living room, and she commissioned a friend, whose visual art talents she alone had any faith in, to paint an entire peacock, in naive art colors, that covered half of the salon wall. That was Noubar, who preferred to waste his talents on solo belly dance presentations, which Persephone watched him rehearse

21

and then helped out on during performances at one of the city's theaters. The vociferous bird with its fan shaped tail may have been one of the rare creative achievements of that young man who unfortunately did not live very long. His body was found thrown down an elevator shaft in a building under construction near his place of residence. Rumor had it that he'd gotten into an argument with a friend who accused him of cheating on him. The medical examiner reported that Noubar most likely died instantly as his friend bolted out of there.

Persephone bought copper pitchers and trays from the flea market on the other side of the capital. She crafted the dining table out of wild cherry wood; one thick slab that showed its grain surrounded by chairs made of white stainless steel. She also restored the radiant gold color to the miraculous icon of Mary Gate of Heaven that she inherited from her mother.

From her window in the morning, Persephone could see the sea. A blue square filling a space between the massive and gloomy Lebanon Electric Company building and a new glass office building whose entrance reflected the light of the rising sun. She filled the gaps in her day reading detective novels—"The Black Series," which she inherited from her father. He had started collecting them early on, with their dark covers and yellow titles, and she carried on the tradition buying new books in the series as they came out. She liked what was written on the back cover: *"Stories with policemen more corrupt than the criminals and a private investigator who doesn't always crack the case. Sometimes there's not even a case to be cracked, or an investigator."*

Apart from reading, she passed the time listening to music or spoiling her twins, Sabine and Nicole, who imitated her, rubbing sunscreen on their tender skin and lying down next to her at the yacht club in their bathing suits and sunglasses. Once a month she would go out for a luncheon with her girlfriends-

schoolmates, with their talk about fish broth, the bouillabaisse at Cocteau Restaurant, with white Alsace wine. They were always chiding her for being so quiet all the time. "Frowning will give you wrinkles, Perso." Their marriages were failing, but their laughter rang out nonetheless.

In the morning, she returned phone calls that she hadn't had the energy to answer the evening before. She watched a freighter ship as it sailed into the Port of Beirut, and if she lowered her gaze, from where she was sitting she could entertain herself watching the workers as they flocked into the press. She sees them, but they don't see her. She can tell who they are by the order of their arrival, and the poorer ones from their clothes and appearance. The ones who work closest to the machines, with their supplies, liquids, and black color, are the earliest to arrive, followed by the administrators, while the graphic design girls always come up the road late and in a hurry. As for the foreman, Anis al-Halwany, friend of the family since his father's and grandfather's time, she never once saw him coming up from the street in the morning, as if he spent nights there at the press.

She thinks about the new young employee with his notebook. He hadn't forsaken his suit and wide red tie during the remaining weeks of the hot season. Rather, he brought in a wooden hanger from home to hang his jacket on. The disparity between the simple job he did and the importance he gave to his appearance while doing it was clear, so when he showed up one day without the necktie and his top two shirt buttons undone, showing some of his thick, black chest hair, one might think that his morale had taken a tumble the night before for some sudden reason and that when he woke up the next morning he didn't have the strength to restore it. He had broad shoulders and didn't look like the other workers at the press. He didn't really look like any other workers, period.

23

5

Farid worked out all the details in his mind. For the front cover of his forthcoming book he chose the famous near-touching fingers of God and man, a section of Michelangelo's *The Creation of Adam* on the ceiling of the Vatican's Sistine Chapel.

For the dedication, he insisted on being concise: *"For me."* On his mother's copy, in nice handwriting, he would write: *"To my lighthouse in this tumultuous life."* Hers would be the only copy he would sign.

After the rude guy at the publisher surprised him with the fact that the title he'd chosen, *The Book to Come*, was already being used in French—a fact he confirmed after a careful investigation of his own—Farid started to lean toward abbreviating. Perhaps he would shorten the name of his masterpiece to *The Book*, for example, plain and simple. And why not? Imagining how the first page would look, he wrote out his name at the top of a blank sheet of paper and sketched the title with large letters. He tried to add a short explanatory label under the title, starting with "Passages," and then "Passage," which he traded in for "Words" and then "Diwan." He even had the audacity to try "Holy Verses" before scrapping the whole idea and going back to *The Book* without anything else.

He might prefer it to be printed on large-size paper, like the size of a church book—like the Epistles of St. Paul he read from at Our Lady of the Angels church and from which he drew conclusions that didn't occur to the parish priest. The first time he'd heard it read was by the priest at his brother's wedding. After that, Farid would read it, projecting his voice as far as possible so it reverberated through the church on Sundays and holidays over the heads of the families celebrating holy mass.

He also wanted his book to be inviolable, bound in signatures with uncut pages, to protect it from the intrusion of nosey browsers who just happened to be passing by the shelf where it lay in the bookstore. Whoever purchased it would need one of those fancy letter openers with an ivory inlay handle to open it, scattering paper dust onto his clothes and into the air all around him.

There wouldn't be any summary on the back cover, because his writing was unsummarizable. It was already the epitome of brevity and precision. He would not allow there to be an excerpt from the book, either. He was not going to give away its linguistic style or themes at first glance. And he wouldn't include his date of birth since he didn't see any advantage to be gained from such an open declaration. He wouldn't cite his father's name or list the various degrees he'd earned and all that nonsense. He only wavered over whether or not he would mention being the heir to the Abu Shaar family—that dubious genealogical relation that haunted him. Finally, he made up his mind. He didn't want to be indebted to anyone, no matter how high his literary prestige rose. He was self-existent, and that was all. The back cover would remain completely unsullied and would not even list the price.

❧

Farid and the Abu Shaar family hailed from a village whose white stone houses outnumbered its fifty inhabitants in winter, compared to roughly six thousand scattered across the two Americas, according to a census by the Lebanese Diaspora Institute. It was small, but its land area within the municipality limits was large, and in past decades was overrun with grapevines that came from France and supplied the wineries on the mountain slope overlooking the Beqaa Valley. The neglected lands of the St. Elias endowment were used for military purposes as well. One day, a group of workers arrived. They looked like soldiers and went to work building a camp that they evacuated overnight. It was for some men and women who arrived in two covered military trucks. Japanese men and women whose shouts in their native language while performing training exercises, such as passing through circles of fire or shooting live bullets over the heads of others advancing toward them on their bellies, reverberated into the town's surrounding hills. Up until one dawn when two Israeli warplanes attacked the camp after two commandos from the Red Japanese Army blew themselves up at Lod Airport in Tel Aviv, killing twenty-six and wounding eighty. A third fighter was arrested. The Japanese militants who were still alive after being subjected to successive attacks by Israeli F-16 fighter jets, left the camp. Some zealous Kurds took their place—men and women again, from the Workers' Party who constituted a support base to fight the Turkish state.

The Abu Shaar family was originally the Shidyaq family. The earliest ancestor was a very handsome man, as people said and as was depicted in charcoal sketches. He was a *zajjaal*[3] oral poet who went from village to village singing his verses, with his long blond tresses dangling loose onto his shoulders. During a year of famine and drought that befell Mount Lebanon, our poet lampooned Emir Abdallah Chehab III, who had been too preoccupied raising pigeons to notice the people's problems. In his poem he delivered two derisive lines that were repeated on people's lips from the towns of Batroun to Wadi al-Taym. So, the Emir summoned him and commanded that his golden locks be cut as punishment to this "Abu Shaar"—Guy with all the hair—for satirizing him, thus giving him the name that stuck with him and all his descendants.

They worked in every type of occupation, but oral poetry and writing remained their natural disposition. They became quite numerous, to the point where Lebanon became too cramped for them, and so they set sail for Brazil. They established March 25th Street in Sao Paolo, and there they bought and sold everything and anything that could be bought or sold. They launched a literary club they named "The Andalusian League." They'd meet there, drink arak, and engage in poetic duels with each other. Those among them who'd been born in Brazil abandoned the Arabic language but continued producing rhymes in Portuguese, nevertheless, until recently. And people say that the great writer who took up the Amazon, its inhabitants, and its nature, as a singular topic for his novels owed his incredible talent to his mother, who hailed from the Abu Shaar family.

Before that, in Cairo, one of the Abu Shaars expertly translated Virgil's *Aeneid* into thousands of metered and rhymed lines of "mistake-free" Arabic verse. His son began translating *The Divine Comedy* into "the language of the tribe of Quraish," as he called it, but he stopped in despair when he reached the inscription over the gates of Hell that said, "*Divine power made me, Wisdom Supreme, and Primal Love. Before me were no things created, but eternal; and eternal I endure. Leave all hope, ye that enter…*" They established schools, published newspapers, and together in Beirut they began compiling a hefty encyclopedia of information and general knowledge that they hoped to be "a dictionary for every specialty and every quest." It lay waste to their years and sapped their strength, but they weren't able to get beyond the letter "*tha*", the fourth letter of the alphabet. The last one to work on it died while in the process of finishing the biography of Abu Mansour al-Nisaburi, one of the most eloquent of the Arab literati, who was nicknamed "*al-Thaalibi*"—the "Fox Catcher"—because his father was a furrier who sewed wild animal skins.

One of them was a man who the Maronite Church excommunicated and put in jail for adopting Protestantism. And so, his older brother left for Damascus while the younger brother banished himself to Egypt where he studied Islamic jurisprudence at al-Azhar and converted to Islam. He was a neighbor to Charles Dickens in London and Gustave Flaubert in France, published a newspaper in Istanbul, and died in Tunisia. They worked in teams of two or three classifying Arabic grammar and organizing it in levels of increasing difficulty, in order to facilitate learning for students. As a result, their family name became synonymous with Arabic language textbooks. Children would come into bookstores at the start of the school year asking for "Abu Shaar, Second Intermediate," or "Abu Shaar Exercises for Fourth Grade." They composed an imitation of the *Maqamat* of al-Hamadhani[4] and tried to revive all the various genres of rhymed poetry—*hija'* (satire), *madih* (panegyric), *ritha'* (elegy). But then their literary output came to a halt for reasons no one could fathom. The new generation, scattered between the diaspora and the homeland, turned their attentions to computer science, marketing, and advertising. One was known to be the owner of an art gallery on the River Seine Street in the sixth arrondissement in Paris, and another was chief of the Arabic-English translators' unit who were dispatched among the various sectors of the U.S. Army at the time of its invasion of Iraq.

Farid completed the book that, for the first time in three decades of barrenness, would carry the name of an author from the Abu Shaar family. He worked hard writing it and did not read any of it to anyone. The day he felt satisfied with it and decided not to add or subtract a single letter, he ended it and took it around to show to publishers. He never parted from it, never left it at home as he did not want it to fall into the hands of one of his brothers and have them read it to each other. He knew they would be astonished merely by the fact that the author Farid was their brother, without delving into the meanings of his writing. He placed it beside him on his desk at Karam Brothers Press, keeping it in sight as he performed his editing work on the various Arabic language materials that came to him.

Despite all that, a day came when he forgot his notebook at the press. It was a day when he had lots of work piled up on his desk, so at the end of his shift he grabbed a stack of files to take home with him and left. If his hands had been empty, certainly he would have noticed the lack of his usual "cargo." The second he realized he didn't bring his manuscript with him, he almost went back to the press right then at night, but he waited until the next morning. When he reached the bottom of the hill, he saw an unusual four-wheel-drive vehicle with military registration blocking the narrow driveway leading to the press.

6

That night when Farid Abu Shaar went home without his manuscript, Persephone woke up, at 2:15 a.m., after tossing and turning all alone in her bed. Her insomnia always seemed to strike just when the regular sleepers were deep in slumber. She would wake up, ready to go, even if she hadn't come to bed until midnight. September was nearing its end, but still the heat prevailed. Light from the garden lamps poured in from the high windows, draping the giant peacock in a kind of suit that looked nothing like its daytime garb. The light flooded the salon and along with it the Bichon Maltese dog that was curled up on the sofa, illuminating everything in harsh colors intensified by sudden flashes of light and zapping sounds from the electric mosquito killer. As soon as she gets up, she relights the stick of incense that her husband would have extinguished before going to bed, warding off the harsh neon lights and her bout of sleeplessness with the scent of sandalwood. She opens the door to her twin daughters' bedroom just a crack, without making a sound, and delights in the sight of them: Sabine, with her leg inadvertently propped against the wall; and Nicole, with the pillow over her head as always to help her fall asleep. She smiles and goes inside to tuck them in. She kisses them and makes sure they're covered well with the lightweight summer blanket.

She goes back into the living room and plops down on the sofa in the corner, out of range of the security camera. She picks up a book and starts reading it. She keeps books scattered around in the corners of the house. She's supposedly reading all of them at the same time. She doesn't shut them or put them back where they belong on the shelves, but rather leaves them open upside down on tables and pillow cushions—her detective novels and picture albums of famous painters or historical cities awaiting her. She instructs Fleur to leave them as they are and where they are. She reads a few lines from *The Blind Man in the Cathedral*, and just like every other nighttime attempt, she feels that books will not soothe her; the words drawn there on the page before her mix and mingle with their meanings, pushing down on her with an unbearable oppressiveness. She stops reading and goes out to the balcony. A cat meows and jumps, fleeing into the darkness. Persephone listens to the sounds of the night, to the baffling jazz music of John Coltrane, ushering in the dawn that won't be long in coming. She enjoys a fleeting cheerful mood that is interrupted by the echo of a machine gun firing in the distance. Popping sounds are accompanied by voices calling out from the bars on the neighboring street. Their music won't quiet down until dawn, when, after all the drinking, drowsiness will finally toss the patrons out.

She wanders back through the corridor between the bedrooms again. Although she has exhausted all of her usual sleepless-night activities, she still doesn't feel tired or sleepy. She heads to the kitchen, drinks some ice water, and opens the little door. Holding her slippers in her hand, she listens a little before going down the stairs to the press. She listens for sounds of employees who might be below working late. It is the second time she goes down there at night, to the long hall of machinery and offices. She is afraid of seeing what she saw the previous time a year or two ago, on a hot night just like this one, or what she imagined she saw.

There had been three men. Light was shining upward on them from below, from lights on the collating table. They were standing around the table engaged in a serious discussion. Folds of shadow and light hit their faces, giving them wrinkles. She saw her father-in-law, Lutfi Karam, and recognized Master Anis Al-Halwany. Between them stood a young man with a woman's voice. She heard him speaking Arabic but didn't understand a word of what he said. He was holding a piece of paper and pointing to the details of the drawings on it. He held it between his thumb and index finger, feeling its texture. He was comparing it to another paper. The three men did not see Persephone because they were standing some distance from the stairs and their eyes were blinded by the strong light; and also, because they were engrossed in the details of those papers strewn before them that they held up to the light, one at a time, and then whispered and nodded their heads. Only the strange young man was speaking, in a raised voice. She could hear some noise and other voices coming from the direction of the big machine, but she couldn't see who it was. She went back upstairs to the house, and from time to time the scene would haunt her. She would see the three men coming out of an old oil painting, conspiring inside one of the royal courts, with long faces and serious stares. Or they'd be with Christ's disciples in Caravaggio's painting depicting the last supper at Emmaus, which she saw at the museum in Milan on a trip with the Fine Arts Academy where the students studied at great length the language of colors and shadows.

The hall this night was blissfully quiet, lit up by the colored power lights that stayed lit on the modern machinery. The whistle of electricity came intermittently, along with the buzz of the cooling fans that never slept. Meanwhile, the sound of John Coltrane's saxophone still reached her ears, accompanied by the yelps of some drunk young men howling at the full moon that shone above the city as Persephone descended the stone stairway, barefooted.

She walked slowly, her bare feet sticking to the floor. She liked the warmth of the tiles, drew it into her body. She runs her fingernails along the metal side of the new printing machine and keeps going until making a turn in front of Dudul's office. Then she returns from the other side like a night watchman securing the area. Suddenly she catches a glimpse of the copyeditor's desk. The new guy's black eyes always lit up when he passed by her during the day. She approaches the desk, inspecting his things, and in the dim light creeping in she sees the red notebook tossed on top of the papers. Here was his secret. The notebook he never parted from. He'd left on it the smell of his body and sweat of his hands. He might have gone home and left it there intentionally. She picks up the manuscript and takes it back to her bedroom.

She goes into the bathroom, washes her feet with soap. They were black from all the grime on the press floor. Her wakefulness had run its course, and now she would be able to get back to sleep. She puts some light dabs of perfume around her neck and under her arms. Then she slowly removes the pink satin nightgown and bra, keeping on only the short, transparent undershirt, which is also pink. She turns on the little lamp on the night table next to her bed and sits up after piling four pillows behind her back. She places the red notebook on her bare knees hugged together. She smiles at the title and the dedication, despite not being able to ascertain their meaning or intention: *The Book;* "*For Me.*" She turns the page and gives it a try. She glides along the surface of the words, not understanding but a few scattered expressions. Nice sounds that have a ring to them but don't add up to anything of meaning. The rhythm of literary Arabic has had an enchanting effect on her ever since that handsome teacher she once had who recited it with a kind of celebratory tone that suited it. That was during the few lessons she attended before deciding to drop Arabic and concentrate on completing a French Baccalaureate. She delighted in listening to Arabic, just as she secretly enjoyed Syriac funeral prayers at St. George's Maronite Church that she attended with her husband whenever a relative passed away. The prayers got through to her via a few familiar expressions here and there. Just like some Urdu songs she guessed were love songs that she didn't understand but revealed meanings to her, which would turn out to be much less significant than she imagined if ever she were to find out what the words really meant, and their spell would be broken. She starts reading the manuscript again and has no idea what she's reading. She keeps trying, but still doesn't understand. She turns the pages written in beautiful script. She notices how beautifully written the letters are, and all have the same height on the line, making them look printed, but somehow the language slips away from them. The words start to dim and the sound of them remains suspended in her imagination…

She peers at the purple curtain, waiting for drowsiness to return. Some echoes reach her from outside. She can no longer resist letting go. She knows sleep is imminent when a certain numbness comes to her, from her head, from behind. How rarely it comes. She doesn't have the power to resist it any longer. She lowers her body, plunges into the bed, and pushes the pillows aside in one final motion, kicking them off with her leg. They scatter onto the bedroom floor on both sides of the bed. She turns onto her right side, lies on her shoulder, and places her arm under her torso the way she always does in her last moments before falling asleep, exposing the dainty lotus flower tattoo on her left shoulder. She moves her legs apart, lets her mind wander a little, thinks slowly about what she might do with this manuscript. She thinks of Dudul's games. If only she could consult him. After a few minutes, she surrenders to her numbness and falls asleep with the red notebook on her pillow.

7

The two policemen Farid saw as he came up the road to the press didn't seem to be on guard. The skinny one was leaning against the wall looking at his phone, reading messages, smiling, and excitedly writing quick replies. His calmer partner had an M-16 on his shoulder and was scoping the area with his eyes through the little jacaranda forest. He, too, hadn't been expecting to find this wide-open space with its burst of purple colors, tomcats, and morning birds right there in the middle of the city.

Their assignment was to prevent anyone from entering the press. The employees had congregated near the trees and were making conjectures about what was going on. They were passing the time reading the expressions on their colleagues' faces as they arrived in succession and confronted the situation. The two repairmen thought it was some sort of prank, and the press owner's secretary, who came up the road in her high heels and tiny footsteps, gasped when she found out what was happening. Her eyes popped, and she put her hand over her mouth to hold back a shriek. She stepped aside to ask her coworkers what was going on but wasn't getting anything useful from them. Finally, Master Anis poked his head out the door between the two security guards. With a calm tone and funereal look on his face, he asked everyone waiting outside to go back home.

"Take the day off!" he said and added that it was just a bookkeeping matter that was being handled, just like two years back.

He reassured them, and reassurance was what they were looking for. One of them, though, who kept up with the newspapers, was surprised to see "Office of Financial Crimes" on the car with the military license plate that was parked in the middle of the street. It was one of four 4-wheel drive vehicles—a brand-new black Ford Explorer. He knew it had been a gift from the American Embassy, a reward to Lebanon for abiding, even if a bit late, by the "dormant" agreed-upon finance standards concerning money laundering. It was no secret from those in the know that tax evasion was the specialty of the Ministry of Finance and its lazy inspectors.

The crowd dispersed. Dozens of workers headed downhill toward parking lots where they'd left their cars for the day, or to catch a taxi. They had an entire free day in front of them that had come unexpectedly, and which they were just beginning to plan how to spend.

Farid Abu Shaar didn't leave. He remained behind, all alone, standing in the shade of the jacaranda trees and holding the files he'd finished editing the night before. After a little while, he loses his patience and takes a step toward the door. The two policemen are unable to come up with a legitimate reason to demand he do as his colleagues had done and leave the premises. Indeed, the crowd of men and women had been less troublesome to them than this obstinate one who kept coming closer and closer, trying to get a look inside at a particular spot he couldn't quite see. Despite his height, he's forced to stand on tiptoes and crane his neck to the right, trying to see inside to that spot. The policemen prepare themselves, taking precautions against any unexpected actions on his part. When one of the noncommissioned officers comes out of the press carrying a large box, the policemen take the opportunity to push the intruder away from the door. Abu Shaar backs up a few meters but remains drawn to the inside, trying his best from afar to peer inside at his desktop covered with piles of papers and files where, somewhere in the jumble, he most likely left his red notebook.

He stands his ground. He waits until the investigators finish having the items they've impounded loaded into their black vehicles. The highest ranking one reprimands the young policeman who's constantly busy with his smart phone. "Enough fooling around, enough romance! You represent the State!"

They leave.

Farid approaches the door. He hears people talking inside. He can't make out what they're saying because of the echo inside that huge space that is so empty now without its employees. He appears in the doorway and the voices go quiet. There are three of them: One is Abdallah Karam, the main boss, standing at the doorway to his office with his shoulder leaning against the door frame. He has one hand in his pocket, and the other keeps stretching the strap of his suspenders forward and then letting it snap back against his chest. Fleur had awakened him at six in the morning, afraid to tell him in her French that the "Police" were knocking at the door and ordered her to wake him up and let them into the press. Dudul was calm, in comparison to the apparent frustration of the others.

Another is Persephone Melki, who had put herself together in a hurry before coming downstairs to see what was going on. She was sitting down, on guard. She had been staring at the copyeditor from the moment he entered and was about to start talking to him. Farid first heard the word "Perso" at the press. He was thinking it must be some new technical term before a question from Abdallah Karam to his secretary caught his attention— "This is Perso's mail. What is it doing here?" He realized then that it was a household name. A week later he discovered it was a pet name for the press owner's wife. He came upon her full name when asked to provide details on an application to participate in a bidding auction for the press. It was on Mr. Abdallah Karam's ID card. His mother's name was Sonya, and he was married to Persephone George Melki. The old calligrapher told him that Beiruti families of Greek origin liked to preserve their ancient names. Farid read in *The Encyclopedia of Greek and Roman Mythology* that Persephone was the daughter of Zeus, god of sky and thunder. She was also called Cora and might even be Venus herself. Here she was before him now, embarrassing him with her glances. She was fresh, clean, her eyes a little sleepy, her short hair glimmering as though she'd washed it and didn't have time to dry it, her dress loose-fitting and simple. She had some white papers in front of her on which she was sketching three-dimensional architectural drawings with a pencil while the anti-financial crimes police raided the press.

The third person was Master Anis Al-Halwany, standing and leaning against a cabinet in a rare moment of silence, with his arms folded, too. Usually he gave the impression he was busy with something. The way his body lurched in more than one direction seemed to indicate he was planning a series of tasks for himself that he'd missed doing that morning which had caused him to tense up with worry over what might happen. He appeared quite knowledgeable about secret things.

Abu Shaar, intent on pursuing his mission, was hesitant to intrude on their meeting. But he didn't see his notebook from where he was standing. He needed to get closer to be certain, but he felt he had walked in on a private conversation. Words were hanging in the air that had been spoken before he entered and would be resumed as soon as he left. He walked around them, advancing toward his desk. The married couple followed him with their eyes: Abdallah, continuing to play with the suspenders he hadn't abandoned since recovering from the explosion; and

Persephone, holding the pencil she had been drawing cubes with, though not drawing anything now. Farid had given them a little break from what they had been in the midst of. He searched the top of his desk and looked inside all the drawers. He leaned down and checked underneath it. He walked all around it and then stopped, studying the area, which prompted Master Anis to say to him, "Maybe they took your notebook with them. Who knows? They took all kinds of things no one would think of..."

"How did you know I lost my notebook?" Farid pointed out perceptively, despite being regarded as a bit of a dimwit.

"It's the first time I've ever seen you without it..."

Persephone stood up abruptly, in an apparent gesture of protest against the underlying sarcasm in Anis's statement, or because she'd suddenly remembered an important appointment. As she turned to leave, some heavy object fell to the floor, making a loud thud more like an explosion—it was a snow globe on one of the page layout designers' desks. Persephone's attention was drawn for a moment, but not finding a compelling reason to turn back, she continued on her way toward the stone steps. She went up the stairway quickly. Her head disappeared first, and then her legs followed behind. Anis went back to his house. He came every day on foot to Martyrs' Square and from there caught a taxi to the outskirts of Lower Basta.

Farid Abu Shaar marched like a soldier over to the Internal Security Administration building, hoping to get his manuscript back. His mind wandered at times to the image of Persephone Melki, or to Persephone of the myth, and other times he clenched his fists in frustration with himself for having been unwilling to save even a photocopy of his book.

Abdallah Karam went inside his office to play poker, Texas hold'em online, in an attempt to take his mind off of the mess they were in. He played every hand he was dealt, even if he had lousy cards, as though he were daring the game itself, until luck smiled on him and he showed his hand after calling "All In." He won the pot with four kings, beating his final opponent from Ohio who called himself "Cincinnati Kid," and who'd dazzled him by getting dealt a straight, five cards in a row. On top of recouping his previous losses, Abdallah Karam won five hundred dollars. He peered outside his office door again, making sure the press was still empty, and then went back to his screen to watch a ten-minute film before shutting the computer down and leaving.

8

Abdallah grew up on word games. There wasn't a single word he couldn't define, to the point where his friends called him "Petit Robert" after the famous French dictionary. He was an authority on riddles and puns, and an expert at solving "word search" puzzles. He met the woman who would become his wife at a Scrabble competition—girlish chatter and prattle in French, a sumptuous dinner, and a radiant young woman with an obscure glimmer of sadness in her eyes that caught his attention. He asked the woman hosting the dinner party for the girl's name and then devised his plan. When it came time for the Scrabble match, he had gathered enough little wooden tiles to spell out her name—Persephone— in its entirety, there in front of him on the game board. Everyone clapped for him and the girl's cheeks filled with color.

After that night, he didn't let up. With the help of an advertising agent who did business with the family press, he rented fifty billboards at a discounted price and without the knowledge of his father who was grooming him to take over the press at the time. He carefully selected the billboards' locations in the quarter where his new girlfriend lived and at the main intersection in the capital as well. Each sign had the same picture printed on it—a hand in a white shirt sleeve with a gold button on the cuff holding a bouquet of flowers. Written above it was the phrase: *White roses for Persephone*. Pedestrians and people driving by thought it must be some sort of ad campaign, and due to the foreignness of the name, imagined it might be for some German brand of washing machines or maybe a line of expensive French lingerie. Persephone saw the ad and knew right away that there was no other girl in Beirut with her Greek grandmother's name who could be the target of that romantic gesture. But she held off believing it was directed at her until the next morning when a delivery man knocked at the door holding the same bouquet of roses pictured on the poster, wrapped in a clear plastic sleeve with her name printed on it dozens of times in a shower of tiny red stars.

Abdallah's future was set for him—he had a good job waiting for him, and he was an only child who would inherit "a fortune," as they said. His name appeared on a list in a magazine article with the title: Ladies, Meet Beirut's Top Ten Eligible Bachelors. He'd had a relationship with another young woman. They dated for months and then broke up without making the reason public. There was a pleasantness about his face and a jolliness to his stocky physique that radiated confidence and made up for what he lacked in looks and elegance. He was always present, never inattentive or in a bad mood. When meeting with friends he listened more than he spoke, about the dangers threatening the country or the folly of its politicians or "that devil residing in the Middle East," as the more eloquent ones would say. He persisted in his antics with Persephone by placing a traffic ticket on the windshield of her car. Inside it she found a love letter constructed from words cut out of newspaper articles and arranged one after another as a way of saying that the owner of a press should use printed letters. In the end, he asked for her hand via text message, which he sent to her cell phone right after they'd left the new sushi restaurant in the commercial center of the capital. She wasn't expecting any message from him at that time, considering they had just parted from each other contentedly. The message was composed in such a manner as to make one think he really hadn't gone to much trouble or tried to get his feelings across in carefully constructed sentences. "The moment I met you, my life turned a new corner. And today I've decided to ask you to marry me, so we can become one before God and men. I love you." It seemed more like something he'd copied from a book on "How to fill out a job application" or "How to write a formal apology" or "How to compose a letter proposing to the girl you love."

She didn't accept his proposal right away. She waited. She waited for feelings of love to well up from her heart, for Abdallah to transform into her hero. They would sit in a secluded corner of a restaurant or spend hours in private in her bedroom, but there was always that wall between them. Abdallah would talk. He'd go overboard talking, actually. He had a real talent for turning every little thing into anecdotes he embellished with details with great ease. She asked him about his relationship with his mother. He smiled and flung his hands wide, not finding the right words, as if the answer was obvious and that a boy's relationship with his mother was the same for everyone. Then he transitioned to talking about his mother's origins and her religious relatives, or the story of his grandmother on his mother's side who owned the house and horse stables. When Persephone dared to question him about what exactly it was that he found most attractive in a woman's body, and whether he preferred making love in the dark or in the light, at night or in the morning, on land or in the sea, he almost got upset for the first time since they started seeing each other months earlier.

After her repeated attempts, she eventually came to believe that what she was looking for was merely a figment of her own imagination. The defect was in her. That was what she heard whenever she complained about her suitors. She didn't find the man of her dreams among those young men her girlfriends dreamed of dating. Or maybe she was asking for things from her suitors that didn't please them or looking for things in a husband that just didn't exist among them. She gave up in the end. The image of her parents came to her. She remembered those long nights, especially during the battles in Beirut and the sounds of intermittent shelling that came and went, getting between them and their ability to sleep at night in their house which was close to the front lines. Her father would spend entire hours reading old newspapers and getting stuck on crossword puzzles while her mother watched TV with the sound muted.

Persephone decided to go ahead and marry Abdallah Karam. He was stocky and rich and entertained her with games and surprises. She decorated his house above the press for him as if it were her own. She wouldn't know how to begin another love story with another man that would end in marriage—something her mother raised her to do as quickly as possible.

Their wedding was elegant and simple, with family and close friends in attendance, but Abdallah topped it off by hiring a Cessna from the Amateur Aviators Club to fly across the sky at the very moment when they came through the doors of the church where the wedding ceremony was held. It had a big banner attached to it with their names on it. They went on their honeymoon, came back, and settled down in the new house above the press. Persephone got pregnant right away, and after the third month the doctor informed her she was "hiding" a healthy set of twins in there. Two girls. And then, on a sunny winter day, Valentine's Day to be exact, the world came crashing down on their heads.

Abdallah was on his way out of a long meeting with the manager of one of the banks in Beirut. They had been discussing the risks of taking on too much debt and a plan for improving the press and the high expenses it would incur, all in light of the unstable security conditions. They tried to determine the amount required to make sure they could import the modern machinery that the Karam family was insistent on buying, and they agreed to hold one final and decisive meeting in a week's time. When Abdallah stepped out the door of the building, heading to his car parked nearby, everything blew apart. He said later on that he didn't hear the explosion, but rather it struck his body without sound and propelled him into the wall. They took him to the hospital, half-dead, his head covered in blood. A piece of shrapnel got embedded in his face and skull, and he suffered a broken shoulder as well. The truck packed with explosives, said to have been driven by a suicide bomber, killed twenty-six and wounded nearly a hundred people.

He survived with great difficulty. His whole body was broken, and his face was disfigured. He became more and more addicted to his computer. He immersed himself in it for hours, having chosen "Gutenberg 9" as his password. He kept all the press's secrets and finances on it. He got swept into gambling—betting on French soccer, American basketball, Scottish horseracing, and even the results of boxing matches. He found a way to kill time with all sorts of games. Letter games, number games. From Sudoku to online poker and from there to a string of porn sites he got addicted to visiting even during the day, during work hours, to the point where people entering his office started to notice how he would turn off his computer all of a sudden if anyone came near his desk.

9

Farid Abu Shaar left the Financial Crimes Department completely dejected. He stood there on the sidewalk outside the administration building like a broken and naked man. The idea of rewriting his book reminded him of the reheated leftovers his mother often tried to persuade him to eat on days when she didn't feel like cooking. He walked aimlessly while trying to retrieve the lost pages from his memory, starting from the beginning. He slowly recited what remained in his mind, in an audible voice and with a fully vocalized and grammatical delivery that drew the attention of passersby. And whenever his memory stumbled, he was overcome by a deep-seated fear, as if the sentence or passage that eluded him had sunk into a bottomless black abyss out of which he could never retrieve it. He headed west, toward the sea, and suddenly heard the sound of an explosion piercing the sky. The blare of a siren ensued, accompanied a few seconds later by another blast similar to the first. An ambulance appeared, impeded by the heavy traffic, led by a black Honda with a man in civilian clothing leaning out the right front window who was intermittently firing a machine gun into the air, one round after another, in an effort to persuade the other cars to make way. The ambulance passed right by Farid. The driver's face didn't show the same terror being promulgated by the gunshots and the incessant siren.

His steps carried him back to Karam Brothers Press, and before going inside, he fixed his eyes on the windows of

Persephone's house, which were flung open in the summer heat. Farid took great care in his manly appearance. He never passed by a mirror without taking the opportunity to make sure he liked what he saw, and his image was as he wanted. He would smooth down his hair or tighten his collar. There was no movement in the upper-level house except for the wind playing with the sheer white curtains that whipped against a cloud of mosquitoes like a rope lashing out in every direction.

He went inside the press and resumed searching the top of his desk to no avail. He was about to start opening the drawers when he heard the sound of a cane hitting the floor tiles somewhere in the distance before the seventy-year-old man producing the sounds appeared, on his way out of the back cellar, with a small book in his other hand. The man was dressed in black, as though he were the dark and mysterious spirit of the place. He pounced on Farid with a question, "What are you searching for, my son?"

"I've only been working here a short time, but I may have lost my most valuable possession!"

"You'll find it. Don't worry. Things around here don't disappear. In fact, they undoubtedly return and reappear. Imagine, just before you came in, I stumbled upon this. It was tossed in a corner in the back cellar. The very first printing of our nation's Constitution. One hundred two articles, in French and Arabic…"

He opened to the last page of the little book and read:

"Effective the 1st of September, 1926, the State of Greater Lebanon shall be called the Lebanese Republic, with no alteration or other modification.

"It will be enacted by this constitutional law, effective immediately upon its publication in the official newspaper.

"Made public in Beirut on May 23, 1926, and printed by…"

He pauses momentarily, to create suspense, and then continues, "Karam Brothers."

"Fuad Karam, the press's founder, set the type for the first Lebanese Constitution with his own hands, by himself, by lantern light at night, after all the workers had left. The directives were to keep busybodies from looking at the founding article before the representative assembly of the Nation of Lebanon voted on it. He arranged the document and redid it several times, separating the pages after dozens of corrections were made and errors in translation were fixed. They tried to avoid copying the Constitution of the Third French Republic verbatim and agreed upon subsequent amendments concerning the necessity of forming an assembly of senators to function alongside the assembly of deputies. Then they backed away from the two-chamber system, only to return to it, putting the responsibility on the ministers, who bore the consequences of their deeds. French High Commissioner Henry de Jouvenel came to the press on the Damascus Highway to speed up the work. "My mission in Beirut comes to an end in twenty-five days," he told them, "and after that I will leave for Paris…"

"He got into an argument with Michel Chiha, member of the council responsible for composing the constitution, who screamed in his face, "You want to make a democratic republic for us, with a parliamentary system that takes into consideration all our private affairs, religious sects, parties, and our political and commercial freedoms, and all within a deadline of three months?"

The man in black wandered about the press, his body lunging to one side while he regained his balance with the aid of his cane and spoke to Farid, whose eyes kept shifting left and right.

"You seem preoccupied. What was it you said you lost?"

Farid Abu Shaar pounded his fist on the desk where he was standing. "One hundred and fifty…! One hundred and fifty-two pages!"

"You will write others. Don't worry. You have your whole life ahead of you, and you look smart."

"But it's a piece of my soul, and I don't have another copy."

"Who around here would steal a poetry manuscript?"

"Did I say I was a poet?"

"No, but you have a look about you…"

Farid couldn't really deny it. He let the man continue.

"…They would come to us clutching their handwritten pages with a lost look in their eyes. They'd pay a small advance and carry their published copies out with them under their arms. I was very lenient with them. I would let them finish paying off the cost of production after selling their books. One of them used to hand his out for free to passersby. They were funny with their obscure writings and strange titles the workers liked to make fun of. *The Fountain of Green Words* or *The Sky Dons an Apron*. A pretty woman came one day with a collection entitled, *I Proclaimed My Love to You*. She was bold. She earned quite a bit of fame, and her book was reprinted several times, but they told me she was unlucky with her husband who cheated on her with the maid…"

He lets out a derisive laugh and comes toward Farid, stepping on some shards of glass scattered on the floor.

"What is this?"

"A snow globe Persephone knocked over." Farid likes saying her name.

It was a snow globe of the city of Beirut. The glass had shattered, and the liquid spilled out; all that was left was the 3-D model that was inside it. It had been modeled on a picture of the nation's capital taken from the air, from the window of an airplane coming in for a landing from the direction of the sea. It showed the seaside hotels—the St. George, the Phoenicia—and to the right the French Boulevard, and after that the buildings of the American University and its green campus.

The man swept the shards of glass around with his cane and asked, "Did Abdallah's wife knock it down on purpose?"

"I don't know."

"What did she say?"

"She was silent."

"Were you at the press when the police came?"

"And who are you?" Farid asks, suddenly putting the question back to the man.

"Lutfi Karam, Abdallah's father. This is my father's printing press. My grandfather Fuad founded it with a lot of toil and trouble. And you?"

"Farid Abu Shaar."

"Did the police ask you any questions?"

"They made us stand outside, all the employees, but I waited until they left."

"Was Abdallah at the press when they arrived?"

"Yes, he was standing here watching them silently."

"And what did they take with them?"

"They took a box, but I couldn't see inside it."

"And you've stayed here since this morning?"

"No. I followed them to the Internal Security station. Maybe they'd taken my book along with the things they confiscated. They sent me over to see an officer with the rank of lieutenant colonel who made it clear to me as he chastised me in a loud and angry voice that they knew what they were doing and that they only take 'suspicious items,' and then he told me to leave."

Lutfi Karam caught wind of the expression and exploded, raising his cane into the air.

"Suspicious items? So now we have suspicious items here? All these years, since the time of the French Mandate, Karam Brothers Press has been entrusted with printing postage stamps and other official stamps, and let's not forget all the tickets for the national lottery. Imagine all that money and all that trust! And the official newspaper, too! We have every issue in the archives in the back, and the provision pamphlets for public auctions, and the official photo of the President of the Republic that is posted in every public office as soon as he is elected, of him wearing the national flag across his chest. We were always the Nation's Press, and now people come here out of nowhere to taunt us while leaving the smugglers and thieves to wander freely. They stick their noses in here hoping they'll find some way to rob us. And what will happen to them if this press is shut down?"

He points to the empty desks and chairs and adds, "Over a hundred employees!"

Then, after calming down just a little, he remembered the obvious question. "And what about you? I've never seen you here before. What do you do?"

"I'm the Arabic copyeditor."

Then he added a tiny lie, his ongoing attempt to improve his image with others.

"...And I translate occasionally."

10

Farid's supply kit included protectors for his white shirt sleeves, enough red Bic pens to fill his pockets, and a resource book on *Common Errors in Arabic Grammar*, by Muhammad Zayd al-Qahtani, which he found in one of his desk drawers. He skimmed through it the first day and didn't find anything useful. But he kept it within reach just in case he found himself faced with some linguistic conundrum.

His predecessor as copyeditor at the press, who was quite advanced in years and whose fingers didn't know their way around a keyboard, either, avoided typewriters in his youth and did not join in the computer craze when they came onto the scene. For years he'd sat at the same desk that was given to Abu Shaar, and then suddenly left. They called him "the Professor." He'd retired from public school teaching, where he "specialized" in fourth-year intermediate level. He lived all alone. He had gotten married, but after a few short weeks his bride ran away and never came back. Her reasons for escaping remained a mystery. His pencil was always tucked behind his ear, ready whenever he needed to make corrections, even to the electric bill whenever he received it—before complaining about the charges. He produced one small publication, which wasn't reprinted, called *A Treatise on Commas and Periods*.

He had been patient about all sorts of mistakes and usage errors he was asked to correct before they went to press, only to suddenly blow up one day without warning. He jumped up from his chair, waving a stack of papers he had been reviewing that had clearly exhausted him. He threw his glasses to the floor, stepped on them with the heel of his shoe, and kept stomping on them until they were grinded to smithereens. Then he crumpled the papers he was holding and tossed them in the waste basket, saying that what was printed on those pages was not words, but fly shit. He asked everyone to bid "*Monsieur* Karam" farewell for him. He said it with malice, in French, for the first and last time. He also asked them to tell Mr. Karam to look for someone else. He never came back to the press a single time after that, not even to ask for wages owed him. He left the press and took up holding regular hours at Hajj Nicola's Café, where the wicker chairs and tables, with their white-and-blue tablecloths, reminded him of his youth. He'd play backgammon and criticize the papers, jeering about all the errors in them. In his desk, he left behind a set of worry beads made of amber stones, some "Arabic" tobacco with a cigarette rolling machine to go with it, and a bunch of keys of different sizes he'd kept even though the only thing they unlocked were doors to houses he'd moved out of long ago.

It was assumed that the press calligrapher would take his place, at least temporarily. That longtime Beiruti began his profession copying Quranic verses people could hang in their houses or shops. He inherited his love for them from his father, the muezzin of al-Omari Mosque. His father woke people chanting Quranic verses, and he wrote them out in beautiful calligraphy. He colored their loops and angles, and embellished them in *al-Ghubar* script on glassware and wood and even gold rings, but suddenly he found himself plunged into copyediting. His first task was to review an Arabic language instruction manual for General Electric refrigerators. He soon discovered that, despite his expert ability to draw *Thuluth* and *Muhaqqaq* script, he didn't know the first thing about controlling the Arabic language. A saying arose that Omar Abdellatif Bazerbashi, who resided on Clemenceau Street in Beirut, was talented at drawing letters and Arabic words, but had no idea about the grammar rules governing them.

He gave up and turned the job over to a woman in her fifties who worked at Karam Brothers. She'd earned a reputation as the "cultured" one at the press because she kept a green chalkboard next to her desk on which, each day, she wrote a famous quote by some world author. In the morning, she volunteered to do the copyediting, and at noon she headed to the office of Abdallah Karam to declare her surrender. The press owner pleaded with her to wait until he could find a new permanent copyeditor.

Farid came the next day, at just the right time, and the woman handed over what she was working on directly to him. She smiled at him and asked if he was on Facebook, or "Book of Faces," as she called it in Arabic—the same place she generally searched for the wise sayings and quotes she came up with. His denial was decisive, and he clearly displayed his ignorance of such things. At any rate, he certainly did not want to open the door for anyone to intrude on his privacy. She backed off without understanding what he meant about privacy; she, on the other hand, was thrilled to announce the birth of her first grandchild on her page and "liked" anyone who commented or shared her feelings. She kept staring in Farid Abu Shaar's direction for some time, even after she'd gone back to her desk. The next day, she wrote a Victor Hugo quote on her green board: "La femme a une puissance singulière qui se compose de la réalité de la force et de l'apparence de la faiblesse." (Woman is a combination of the truth of strength and the appearance of weakness.)

In addition to his ignorance of computers and social media, everything about Farid Abu Shaar's appearance, despite his not yet having reached thirty, screamed old-fashioned. This didn't go unnoticed by Mr. Abdallah Karam the day he received him in his office for the first time, and Farid lost hope of publishing his book once again. The suit he wore was made of checkered grey wool, the kind one can only find at a tailor in one of the inner neighborhoods who'd had the good fortune one day of buying some fine English wool at a cheap price and set about persuading his few customers to let him dress them in this "pure" wool of his. And then there was the wide red necktie, the part in his hair, and the natural formality with which he spoke, as though he were reading out of an old classic. Dudul asked him if he was "good" at Arabic, and Abu Shaar answered like someone who'd just suffered a terrible insult, that he "was born into the language of Bani Taghlib." The heir of the printing press grasped his meaning without fully understanding the reference to the ancient Arab tribe who founded the famous poetry competitions of Souk Okaz and supported early on the Messenger of God.

The day he was asked to be a copyeditor, it was assumed that Farid would refuse outright, but he wavered a little and considered his living conditions. He was living with his mother, the last one to remain with her there in his parents' apartment after both of his brothers had gotten married and settled down with families. She spent a good portion of her savings on him but denied it in front of his brothers. She would say he was the one giving her money, not the other way around, because he was working and was earning an income. Farid worked off and on for very little pay. He posted a flyer on shop windows and bookshops in Furn al-Shubbak where he lived, offering private tutoring for schoolchildren. It didn't take long before the phone calls started coming from parents complaining about their children's poor grades. He'd go to their homes to give lessons to their children who took their time opening their book bags and notebooks, behaved disrespectfully to him as they completed their assignments, and left him feeling guilty if they failed their final exams.

He asked for some time to think it over, which made Abdallah think Farid was trying to negotiate a salary, and so, out of his dire need for a copyeditor, he made him a very attractive offer. But Abu Shaar insisted on some time, if even for the sake of his pride. He spent a whole week getting over what he considered to be an affront to his talents. He headed to his village where he spent two days trying to make up his mind while standing on the balcony of his house, contemplating the changing colors of the plain stretched before his eyes. He returned to Beirut and extinguished his distress and indecision for that one night at "Los Latinos" nightclub with the sexy and friendly blonde who always conveyed to him in a mixture of languages she didn't speak that she preferred him over all the other customers. The next morning, he went back to the press and accepted the job, determined to uncover the secret of the woman who smoked and read and looked directly into strangers' eyes.

He started the job convinced that what was happening to him was only temporary. He did not see himself in that job. For a long time, he tried to hide it from his mother and brothers and friends. When the question, "Where are you working?" came up, he curtly answered, "At a press," cutting the conversation short. If the person pushed for more, he would say he was a supervisor and manager, or even editor, avoiding at all costs the term "copyeditor."

He started the job and despite his age quickly earned the nickname "Professor Farid," owing to the desk he inherited and also because of his composure and expert command of the Arabic language. He quickly discovered what everyone at the press knew, which was that the work of the press depended on him, or whomever sat in his place. Every page proof, every design—every single thing, before it could continue on its way to the huge machines, had to pass by him, had to be "checked," edited, and stamped with his approval that it was "fit to print."

11

Everything meant everything.

Farid proofread everything, from directions to be printed on medicine containers that came to him already translated from local distribution companies, like "Xatral XL," a drug for symptomatic treatment of benign prostatic hyperplasia; to dosage instructions such as "take one pill of the progesterone blocker Mifepristone, and after 24 hours place four tablets of Misoprostol under the tongue for 30 minutes, after which you can swallow your saliva," to a detailed description for the treatment of hemorrhoids using bee honey. Immediately following it, on the very same day, came the task of proofing details and operating instructions for a shipment of AS332M Super Puma helicopters sent by France to the Lebanese Military, in defiance of Israeli objections to the deal. Abdallah Karam himself hand-delivered that one to Farid in a sealed envelope marked "Top Secret," and warned Farid to return it to his office before leaving the press. Then there were the trilingual restaurant menus and the classified ad circulars, in which he failed to find a job opportunity any better than the one he was currently doing at Karam Brothers, and ads for furniture people were trying to sell before moving out of the country, ads offering private piano lessons, ads for companies with branches in the Arabian Gulf seeking attractive young women to fill secretarial positions. There were death announcements and wedding invitations, the guide to Beirut's nightlife, a booklet entitled, "One

Hundred Simple Ways to Prevent Alzheimer's and Senility," contracts for car insurance and life insurance with tiny print they say is done intentionally so clients will sign without reading the details or asking questions. Then there were the magazines, like *Al-Jamaal* (Beauty) and *Al-Shabb al-ʿAsry* (The Modern Man), and *Anaqatuki* (Your Elegance), whose glossy photos printed on expensive paper gobbled up the texts. Articles on "The Perfect Body in Just 10 Minutes a Day," "The Complete Guide to Female Fertility," and "How to Have Sex While Pregnant," or "Your Pathway to Guaranteed Profits," or "How to Make Money Buying and Selling Stocks at the Right Time." A hundred different things for infants and children, knitting catalogues…

Farid Abu Shaar plunged into the task, accepting it without complaint. The heavy strokes of his pen as he crossed out all those errors were the best way to express his disdain of the texts he worked on as well as his scorn for their anonymous authors. This was clear from the way he headed to the bathroom sink four or five times a day and the excess amount of soap he slathered all over his hands as though stemming from a desire to cleanse himself of the "stupidity" of what he was working on and not just the black ink that rubbed onto the back of his hands from constant contact with newsprint. Despite all that, he worked with a rare zeal. Whenever the delivery girl passed by and dropped another "proof" on his desk, he threw himself into it, without raising his head from it, not stopping until he was finished. And if work piled up on his desk that was time-sensitive and had to get to press ASAP, but he was unable to finish copyediting all of it during his shift at the press, then he would take it home with him—papers stacked on top of his literary notebook that he never parted with. He'd go over them while eating his supper in front of the television on which his mother watched her Turkish drama series, "Love for Rent," and gave him her blessings while complaining about her chronic pain.

Or sometimes his papers would go with him to "Los Latinos," a name which had no resemblance to the place. Its patrons were strictly Arabs—Muslims and Christians—and the young women were all blonde and blue-eyed, hailing from cold Slavic countries. There, under the dim lights and amid the din of the loud pop music, a university student who frequented the place and claimed to be an expert on the Arabic language had his curiosity roused. He was always blinking, as if he was winking at someone all the time, and butting in on Farid's work, asking all sorts of questions about the nature of his job and how much he got paid. Farid got extremely annoyed by his behavior and thought, with his constant winking, that he was conspiring against him with the others. When he imposed himself and objected to one of Farid's corrections, Farid rebuked him, quoting straight out of an old grammar book.

"The verb causing its cognate to be declined in the accusative case is necessarily curtailed if the gerund is present in place of the verb, or if it is introduced as a further detailing of what immediately precedes it, or when the gerund refers to a proper noun, or if another gerund comes immediately after it, or if the gerund is a reiteration of itself!"

And with that, Abu Shaar blasted the nightclub student into silence and taught him to quit sticking his nose where it didn't belong.

His choices were definitive concerning what are known as common mistakes, and he sneered at attempts to pass them off in newspapers and novels. No sooner would he finish an editing job that cost him a "white night" during which he barely slept two hours than he would arrive at the press the next morning only to find a new file waiting for him even thicker than the one he'd just finished. He'd press his lips together in disgust until he came to the realization that what he was up against was an unstoppable sea. He saw this sea in his dreams—an ocean whose waters had a greenish color and whose crashing waves on a stormy day were crowned not with foam but with a thick mass of linguistic mistakes shining on top. It was a sea dotted with *hamzas* on top of *alifs* (أ) and below *alifs* (إ), reflexive verbs and transitive verbs, direct objects and nouns functioning as verbs, and numbers expressed in the archaic form, "two and ten" or "eight and thirty after one hundred," and the sounds of the vocative particle mixed with rebukes and cries for help…After a while, he came down with a sort of "mistake fever." He saw them everywhere—on billboards, political posters, business signs. Whenever one would appear to him in the distance, he nearly crossed it out with a motion of his hand, just as he did to all those misplaced *hamzas* (ء) he scratched out with his red Bic pen.

The pressure of his job weighed down on him, and his despair grew after losing all hope of finding his manuscript, which he had been clinging to while indulging himself in the belief that it would be published at Karam Brothers as soon as he established a good relationship with the owners. After a while, coming to the press turned into forced labor that he succumbed to, an income that warded off hunger. A while back, he'd bumped into an old university colleague and poured out his heart to him. He found that lowly job unacceptable for Farid, with no possibility for advancement. His friend promised to help him publish some articles in a journal and tried to make him feel better, telling him he would have a promising future in journalism. In this way, the longer he stayed at the press, the more his job transformed into a harrowing ordeal. He could have gone to Abdallah Karam's office, excused himself from the job in a decisive tone, claiming he was going on a trip or found a more suitable job, but there was another string that tied him to that place. It tugged him to it from the first day and kept reeling him back. The only moment of escape from the tedium of his day-to-day activities was when Persephone came down the stone steps and lit up the hall with her smile, which he thought was directed at him and him alone. In everything she did, he found the promise of another chapter, which kept him on guard, with eyes in the back of his head, watching her every move. Her presence in close proximity to him, or even his knowing she was at home, upstairs, became a force that kept him in his chair, bent over her image, hoping for the chance to catch new signals that brought him closer to her, something that let him get through the day and finish his ever-increasing proofreading work.

But Farid Abu Shaar was not destined to leave the cellars of Karam Brothers printing press so easily. Months after his manuscript vanished without a trace, during which he hadn't been content with a single line he tried to rewrite, he came to work one morning to find a new book on his desk he thought must have been put there by mistake. He put off opening it, pushed it aside, and got started on his work. He copyedited for two hours, got up to go to the bathroom, washed his hands and splashed some water on his face, and came back to his desk, refreshed, only to find the book placed in front of him again, right on top of his papers. He looked around, searching for the secretary who always brought him proofs to ask her what the rush was on this book. He didn't find her anywhere around, so he opened it, noticing right away the unusual feel of the paper. It wasn't like the paper of most books. It was thick and difficult to bend, as if it was wax-coated. He opened to the first page and suddenly realized he was reading his own book. There before him was the first sentence of his manuscript.

He was struck with vertigo by the retrieval of that opening line that was etched in his being and for whose sake he had torn dozens of sheets of paper to get just right. He knew the importance of beginnings. He stood up from his chair, continuing to read and making sure he was really standing before his writings, that they were really right there in front of him in exactly the form he had wanted for them. He looked around himself to see if anyone was watching him or toying with him. He nearly voiced his surprise and ponderings aloud. The atmosphere in the press was business as usual. All the employees were in their regular spots. He noticed that Master Anis had come down to the calligrapher Bazerbashi's office. He braced himself for the possibility the two of them were going to be talking about him, because al-Halwany was looking at him out of the corner of his eye with an obscure smile on his face.

12

A nis, the son of Mustapha, son of Abdelhamid al-Halwany, with emphasis on the "y," the way Beirutis from the Basta quarter pronounced it among themselves, was descended from a long line of talented artisans. They worked hard and didn't acquire much. To the point that Anis, the last of the line, didn't fear war returning to the neighborhoods of Beirut and the absence of any semblance of a state as much as he feared new rent laws being ratified in the Parliament. That would lift the old rent caps and cause rents to skyrocket so high that he and his family wouldn't be able to continue living in their place on al-Nasrawi Street in lower Basta and would be forced out to some unimaginable place.

Abdelhamid, the grandfather, worked at Karam Brothers from the day it was founded. He taught Fuad Karam and his assistants how to operate the press, but the two men were always arguing and getting angry over little things. They had a clash of personalities. Whenever Abdelhamid became disgruntled, he would go work at the Jesuits' Press. Then he would come back to Karam Brothers after the two of them met up at some café in Burj Square and made up with each other. Truly, it pierced Fuad deep in his heart that the day Abdelhamid al-Halwany died they were at odds over some issue he couldn't even remember.

"My grandfather was cheated," his grandson Anis would say as he escorted whomever he was talking to to the back storeroom at Karam Brothers where all the company's artifacts were kept.

He never began telling the story of Abdelhamid without picking up one of the Arabic letters inlaid on wooden squares.

"And what is this?" he would ask before answering his own question. "It's the letter *alif* with double *fatḥa* diacritics above it (آ). And here's the *alif* with the *hamza* beneath it(إ). Before that the diacritics were typeset in separate pieces from the letters."

His grandfather had invented that—the letter with the diacritic together in one mold. He didn't know why the Jesuit fathers called it the "Istanbul font" when they claimed to have originated it. Father Louis Cheikho disregarded Abdelhamid al-Halwany in his book on *The History of Printing and Printing Presses in Lebanon*, but his grandfather was an honorable man who didn't turn on those he worked with.

During the last days of the Great War, a Turkish officer and some soldiers came to the house and waited for Abdelhamid to come home in the evening. They ordered him to come with them, but he told them he never caused anyone any harm and he was one of the Sultan's upstanding subjects. They argued with him, and when the officer failed to persuade him to come with him, he suddenly slapped a charge of treason on him, for working at the Press of the French Jesuits, enemies of the Sultanate. They told him the State required his services, to oversee seizure of the Catholic press. Abdelhamid held his ground, and for years his wife told the story of how the officer, after giving up trying to convince him with words, resorted to hitting him with the butt of his rifle, knocking his tarbush to the ground. Some local residents of the quarter gathered around when they heard the commotion, so the soldiers restrained them. They took Abdelhamid by military escort at night. His wife thought she would never see him again. But he returned at dawn and told her that they'd seized the horse carriages in Beirut and put them in his service for transporting the Catholic press's machinery to the train station in Karantina for delivery to Damascus, per orders that came down from Jamal Basha. Furthermore, they might require him to be forcibly escorted to assemble and operate the equipment there. However, al-Halwany was very clever and pretended to cooperate with them. When he asked for compensation, they assumed he was open to bribery, and so they let him go back home without a security guard. Anis didn't know what happened with his grandfather that night, but he preferred to say that Abdelhamid al-Halwany could not bear the thought of helping the Turks burglarize the press he worked in. It was just as likely to believe that his wife's tears and fears over his leaving to Damascus made him refrain from helping the troops, and instead he left the house at night, despite the dangers in those days, without telling anyone what he planned, not even his wife. It was never known what happened afterward, but no one came to ask about him in the morning, due to the fact that Beirut was embroiled with news that the war had come to an end and the Allies had been victorious over the Turkish Army, which hastily withdrew from the city a few days later.

Anis took over the "trade" from his father Mustapha early on. Abdelhamid had begun by making the molds for the letters, whereas Mustapha specialized in arranging them. He also began working at Karam's, until he was no longer needed. He was difficult and hot-headed. He had his own special system for lining up the letters and their boxes on the shelves. He placed the sun letters—such as the dāl (د), dhāl (ذ), ṣād (ص), ḍād (ض), on the highest shelf, and below it in parallel boxes were the moon letters like ḥā' (ح) khā' (خ), mīm (م), and hā' (ه). That was his invention.[5] If he was absent or left work for some reason, the replacement typesetter found it extremely difficult to acclimate to the unique setup.

Mustapha al-Halwany was, as people said, "a sight to see." He was the fastest typesetter in Arabic, hands down. In his youth, he competed in a contest that took place in Cairo at which he dazzled the judges and received a long round of applause from the audience. He would take the metal ruler and its corner piece in his right hand, stand before the letter cabinet, and take off as if in a fight to the death. He didn't look at the pieces and very rarely did he make a mistake picking up the letters, as long as they were in the windows he had designated for them. The *tā'* (ت) in all its forms—isolated form (ت), tied form (ة), shortened form at the beginning of a word (ﺗ), the final form (ﺖ); the *alif* in all its configurations—from the ones with *hamzas* at the beginning (أ), in the middle attached (ﻟ) and unattached (ا), the *hamza* sitting on the seat of the *yā'* (ﺋ) or the *wāw* (ؤ) or hanging in the space alone (ء) all the way to the final long *alif* (ﻟ) and the *alif maqṣūra* (ى). In addition to the vowel diacritics, there were the commas, and the *kashida* extension lines used to center the line or justify it. He corrected texts as he saw fit, without going back to their owners or even their authors, if he felt there were errors. He used little slivers to adjust the height alignment of certain letters. He'd stick them in to make the letters line up correctly. Then he would press down on the page with the vise and shout to the press worker, "Let her roll!"

The disaster happened the day the book, *Sunun al-Tirmidhi*, one of the six *Kutub al-Sittah* hadith collections, containing the sayings of the prophet Muhammad, went to press and he was out sick with a bad chest cold that had rendered him bedridden. The pages of the last section came apart, and one of the workers volunteered to put the letters back in their places. He set about dropping them into the squares using the standard alphabetical order of handset presses, so the letters got all mixed up. Mustapha came back to work and as soon as he touched them he immediately discovered there was something wrong with the arrangement. When he found out what happened he blew up.

Then he sat in a corner and cried, reminding the press owner that he had warned him not to let anyone work in his place.

No one would ever replace him, because his trade was on the road to extinction. The modern monotype printing machine didn't take much away from him, but the inventions that followed completely wiped out hand set letterpress printing. Each time a printing press became equipped with the new technologies, Mustapha al-Halwany would find himself out of work. Then the owners of the remaining small presses would scramble to hire him, despite his difficult personality, purely for his speed. If any criticism was directed at him that he didn't like, for being late to work for example, he'd throw whatever ruler and letters were in his hand onto the worktable and head out the door, never to return, despite all the boss's apologies and pleadings. He ended up a poor man working in a poor press that specialized in ads printed on flimsy paper handed out to passersby or thrown in the streets, print jobs that got obliterated over time, and some death notices.

In his turn, Anis learned how to set type and mastered the skill at Karam Brothers Press, where his father had begun bringing him from age ten. He worried about his son ending up unemployed, so he pushed him to become good at operating the linotype machine, his arch enemy and the cause of his demise. He introduced him to Lutfi Karam when the press was still located in Gemmayze, and Anis worked for him his whole life and became his right-hand man. He never missed work except during the two years when the capital city was divided because of the war. Anis's place of residence was on one side, and the press was located on the other. He worked hard in more than one press-related skill, but he surrendered before the laser printing machine, after which a flood of new inventions and applications came rushing in, one after another. With the onset of the digital revolution and the spread of little USB drives, he became something like a deaf man at a noisy wedding celebration. The texts arrived already set to print, the machines cut the paper to size and bound and processed them. There was nothing left for him to do in the press but usher in each new development with Abdallah, who considered him a relic from a lost time, or a blessing, the time of machines that blasted ink and left traces of it on his clothes and skin and blackened fingertips. Anis recorded what he wanted to remember in a thick little notebook he pulled out of his pocket whenever he wanted to write down phone numbers or other important things. He gradually lost the ability to contribute anything useful in terms of running machines or overseeing their output, and eventually Anis transformed into Lutfi Karam's "eyes" among the employees, and likewise for his son Abdallah after him.

13

Anis al-Halwany was Abdallah's eyes and keeper of his and his father's secret. He came into Abdallah's house unannounced, played with the little girls. He made them giggle with his funny accent and antics. The little dog would follow him whichever way he turned and get underfoot, causing him to trip. He flipped through the fashion magazines scattered about the living room while waiting for Persephone. She put him in charge of things she wouldn't entrust to anyone else. He could ascertain her mood in the morning from the tone of her voice, even before she appeared, coming out of her bedroom without finishing putting on her makeup. Al-Halwany always prepared himself for the worst.

After Abdallah's explosion accident, al-Halwany became the Karam family's representative. When Abdallah was undergoing risky surgeries, his father Lutfi would stay glued to the hospital waiting room for long, nerve-wracking hours, after turning over the office to Anis al-Halwany. With his penchant for minute details, he was able to handle some business matters decisively, also owing to his skepticism of the numbers presented to him, as though he was not on the same footing with the other employees who poked fun at his seriousness and looked at him with strange, wry glances. During his brief stint behind the boss's desk, he received a phone call from the bank. The woman on the phone informed him in a flat voice that the Karam Brothers Press account was overdrawn and the owners of the establishment should contact the bank administration as soon as possible. When he asked with humble curiosity how much it was overdrawn, she replied that these matters were only to be discussed with the concerned parties, and certainly not over the phone.

The doctors summoned the family, having decided to wake Abdallah out of the coma he'd been in for over two months. He muttered and spoke in a weak voice. His head was wrapped in bandages. He asked for some water to quench his thirst. He recognized everyone, one by one, and asked quietly what he was doing there. They told him he'd been hurt in an explosion, thus making him the last person to find out about the assassination of the prime minister, and that he himself had been one of the unintended victims of that attack, as well as one of the eyewitnesses whose statement would be taken by the investigating judge, even if he didn't have much to say about what happened. He remembered after a little while that his wife was pregnant with twin girls. She told him they'd been born and were waiting for him, so they could baptize them and choose their names. And she told him how she'd put a gold anklet around one of their ankles to tell her apart from her sister, which made him smile for the first time. His parents were brimming with optimism about the possibility of a full recovery. Unable to contain their tears, they rushed out to the hallway, while Persephone stayed beside her husband in the hospital room, getting to know him all over again.

They inserted a nickel pin in his shoulder, after removing the upper joint of his humerus and replacing it with a prosthetic shoulder blade. They sewed up his cheek with numerous surgical stitches after grafting some flesh from his thigh. They told him the scar on his face would remain visible for years. The most difficult surgery was the extraction of a piece of shrapnel that was lodged in the frontal lobe of his brain, between the caudate nucleus and the lentiform nucleus. It was a ten-hour surgical operation that required widening the opening of the skull and cutting a flap in his scalp shaped like a horseshoe. After that, the doctors couldn't determine the damage the shrapnel caused and what effects it would have on "high-level brain functions" until he regained consciousness and went about his normal life activities for one month. After that they would be able to make an assessment and give a prognosis.

The put him back together, beautified him, covered his right cheek with a bandage, and sent him home—to the guest room, per his request, to lighten his wife's burden as he said in the beginning. They brought in a nurse to care for him during his long convalescence. Sometimes Fleur would bring Sabine and Nicole in to see him during the day. He would kiss their feet and tickle them until their laughter filled the room. Friends visited him, and they went over the events together, predicting what the American position would be and lamenting the withdrawal of bank deposits and the plummeting real estate prices. They kept their eyes on proclamations coming out of Iran and expected there to be a few "difficult months," after which tensions would ease. A burly man came to see him who they called "Abu Husein." He told jokes and laughed out loud at them before anyone else. His visit was of some importance to Abdallah. He was accompanied to the house by Master Anis, and a call was made to Abdallah's father Lutfi, who also knew the man, asking him to join in welcoming and chatting with him.

Persephone was sitting with him and had started reading him a chapter from the novel, *The Black Dahlia*, when a terrifying boom interrupted her reading. She went out to the balcony where the employees had already gathered and were looking at the black cloud that had formed two or three streets over to the east. A half hour later, a live news broadcast came on television, from the spot where the explosion had occurred, talking about how the well-known journalist, who had received countless death threats if he continued writing his weekly editorial, was turning the key of the ignition of his Volkswagen when a bomb that had been planted on the car's chassis suddenly exploded, blowing him to pieces and killing the grocer who had been standing outside his shop across the street under a stem of bananas.

✽

Abdallah's stage of private care came to an end, and so, with a tinge of the euphoria of victory, the surgeon declared his patient to have made a complete recovery and regained all his physical and mental capacities. The nurse left, but Abdallah preferred to stay in the guest bedroom, forming the basis of a rumor that went around that Abdallah Karam had fallen in love with his nurse because his wife didn't take proper care of him during his time of hardship. Her attentions were taken up, so they said, by caring for her twins and trying to wean them from breastfeeding.

The truth was that it had become a rarity during the day for her to enter the guest room where he'd been holed up. After so many weeks, she stopped even pushing on the door. She would send Fleur in to tell him about important matters, such as pending visits from relatives or friends, invitations to social occasions they couldn't decline, or the necessity to send an apology for not being able to attend the ones they could decline. The day the two engineers who'd come specially from Germany to install the modern digital printing machine finished their work, Abdallah Karam decided to get out of bed and go downstairs to the press. He asked Persephone to join him at a reception that Master Anis organized, and she accepted.

For the first time since the accident, with his father at his side, he appeared to his team of employees. He was pale, with a wound on his face that was impossible to hide and was dressed in a brown monk's robe tied with a rope at the waist, with the hood thrown back, and wearing open sandals on his feet, without socks. In the peak of fear for his life, when Doctor Ghusn, a graduate of McGill University in Canada and personal physician to the King of Saudi Arabia and a large number of sheikhs and emirs of the Arabian Gulf, who was renowned for making advances in neurosurgery and the search for a permanent cure for epilepsy, stood there perplexed before his parents and his wife, giving them the impression he was not exactly knowledgeable about what he was saying about Abdallah, and informing them about the American method for determining a life expectancy rating on a hundred point scale—amid all that confusion, his mother's relative visited them—Sister Bernadette Baby Jesus, president of the Convent of the Holy Family in Beirut. She offered them something that Lutfi Karam's pious, Maronite wife, who had steadfastly followed all the rules of religiosity since childhood, was incapable of refusing at that moment. And that was to make a vow that if her only son lived to stand again on his own two feet and returned to a normal life, then for an entire month he would wear the robes of the holy monk Saint Anthony the Great.

They greeted him with a round of applause. They served frozen desserts and baklava that one of the employees had brought from Tripoli that morning. One of them recited *zajal* poetry and one of the cleaning ladies let out a long ululation wishing *Khawaja*[6] Abdallah good health and a long life. Their welcome of him mixed with their joy at having achieved their first "test proof" using the new machine. The person in charge of archives opened a bottle of fine champagne, and one of the page designers stuck an icon of Our Lady of the Seas on the metal housing of the Heidelberg, the most advanced digital press in all the Middle East. It worked in five colors, was thirteen meters long, and had a 47.24 x 63.78-square-inch printing format. It was equipped with metal stairs and screens for observing the details of its work and adjusting all of its calibrations.

Master Anis was astounded by its massiveness, and after hearing before its arrival all the praise for its exceptional printing production capabilities, he was never very far away from it. He took personal responsibility for guarding it. He observed what came out from inside of it, inspected the colors, cleaned it of the tiniest specks of dirt, put his ear against it listening to its sounds, and tried in vain to compare its functions with what he had experienced with previous machines. And at home in the evening, he would take great pleasure describing it to his wife over dinner, telling her joyfully that a genie had set up a tent for himself inside of it.

14

At the end of the day, Farid Abu Shaar picked up that precious book of his that had descended onto his desk as if by an angel who had flown off with his manuscript and then come back to drop off the printed version. He carried it home, turning all the pages in succession making sure everything was there.

He didn't know who to turn to about the situation he'd found himself in. If he tried to tell anyone what happened, no one would believe him. Farid knew his nasty colleagues at the press were always laughing at him behind his back. He wished he had just one more copy, so he could give it to his mother. She would certainly take the time to read it carefully while he wasn't home. With that keen intuition of hers she would be able to perceive the meaning of his writings while sitting out on the balcony, which is where he found her when he got home early from work. She had her head in the shade and the rest of her body in the sun while she knitted a little sweater for one of her grandchildren in time for the coming winter. She wouldn't be interested in his problem now, though, being so busy with endless jobs in the kitchen.

He went into his bedroom, shut the door, and delved into his book, reading his words as though he didn't recognize them in their new garb. He recited them out loud and swayed with emotion. The sentences gave rise to new revelations that hadn't occurred to him before. Suddenly the thought came to him that what he was holding so delicately in his hands might actually have been written by hand, which might explain why this lone copy had appeared. He thought to himself that everything that had been going on these past days might well have been the handiwork of the press calligrapher who had been so proud a few days earlier to tell him he'd been chosen to write Quranic verses in calligraphy on the Muhammad al-Amin Mosque. He remembered the way he made a beeline to his desk, his face beaming with the news.

"You asked me about Greek names. There are girls named Aphrodite, Minerva, Athena, and Apollonia!"

He extended his list to Italian names, and Turkish and French, until flashing a sly smile and saying, "But Persephone is the most beautiful of all the names, hands down."

Farid ran his fingers along the sharp edges of the book's paper. He caressed its pages, tested their shininess under the light of the electric lantern, eventually noticing the exact likeness of repeated characters, especially the *qāf* (ق) and the *lām-alif* (لا). He felt certain that no calligrapher was capable of making such exact repetitions. The book had to have been produced by a printing machine. His doubts led him back to the very beginning. The remaining copies were sure to appear unexpectedly out of nowhere.

He tucked the book inside his jacket and hailed a taxi to Los Latinos on the outskirts of the Armenian Quarter. The nightclub would have quieted down after a busy weekend.

❦

His friend Ayyoub, owner of Los Latinos, was a native son of the same Beqaa village and was Farid's inseparable summertime buddy there. Ayyoub spent one month in "the mountains" with his grandmother, while the city swallowed him up the remaining months of the year. He'd been an expert since adolescence at wooing women. He began implementing his ploys at the young age of fifteen. He would tell his awestricken friends, who knew nothing of the city or its goings on, about his adventures, and they would believe every word and fantasize. He sized women up starting from the heel. If the heel was thin and the bone was protruding, then its owner had a strong appetite for sex. As for the girl standing on a fat, rounded heel, she would be prudish and hard to "get." When Farid disagreed with him, Ayyoub would answer sharply that each person had his particular specialty.

"I never argued with you about literary matters or about writing, so leave female matters to me!"

He bid farewell to his village at the age of twenty-five in his own special way. He appeared just before sunset, driving a red convertible corvette with bucket seats, with a girl of indeterminate age whose beauty could not be assessed on account of the big dark sunglasses covering a large portion of her face sitting beside him in the passenger seat. He'd taken her on a little outing to Baalbek, and on the way back he took a detour through the town, touring through its roads before disappearing for good this time, through winter and summer.

He inherited his father's inn in Beirut, which in the beginning had been a destination for not-so-well-off people from Damascus. Some of the young locals from Beqaa villages also frequented it when they were forced to stay overnight in the capital. The place developed a questionable reputation when travelers stopped coming to Beirut while it was inflamed with military confrontations and militants were seen carrying their weapons openly as they went up to their rooms with "cheap women" in tow. And the man sitting at the reception desk, after calm returned or even during the war's various tours through the city, would approach customers to offer them "girls" at reasonable prices.

Farid ran into him by chance years later and wouldn't have recognized him if Ayyoub hadn't spoken up and introduced himself. His bad appearance and early baldness caught Farid's attention. And those glances he used to flash at women to charm them had lost their fire. He'd opened a nightclub in the same neighborhood where his father's inn was located and called it "Los Latinos," after a club he liked in Barcelona. He advised Farid to come on Mondays when the place was practically empty, and the women's prices were lower. Farid forgot all about the invitation, never imagining himself frequenting such a place, until he read a poem translated from Persian in which the poet said:

> Nothing but the purple snow-flower has enchanted me
> And never have I found love but with those love-selling ladies

That encouraged him, and so he decided to pay a visit to Ayyoub's nightclub. Ayyoub guided him toward the more educated women, one in particular he'd seen reading a book in her native language between customers. He asked her what the title was. "The Brothers Karamazov," she replied. Farid grew to feel shy whenever he would run into her. He'd smile at her, feeling a sort of humility between them that transcended whatever had compelled her to come to that part of the world and that had begun to captivate him in that place. The young woman was not aware of her apparent difference from her colleagues in the profession who weren't in the habit of reading. She merely behaved the way her work dictated and didn't give much importance to Farid Abu Shaar sitting at an isolated table, not coming near anyone, since Ayyoub had promised him new pretty ones—ten of them he was going to import soon, one of which he would surely like.

Farid's meetings with Ayyoub became a weekly occurrence. They exchanged news about what had transpired during the seasons of their lives since being separated. Ayyoub told Farid about how he'd fallen in love with one of the women and almost married her, but she refused and went back to her country. He knew everything about that world of hers and said many in Beirut chased after those women. When Farid informed him he'd started working at Karam Brothers Press, Ayyoub was quick to say with confidence that the owner was a regular customer who went from "call girl to call girl." When Farid objected, saying the man wasn't in his best shape, Ayyoub replied that he knew what he was talking about and also knew the man had been gravely injured, but he accused Farid of living outside the real world and not knowing what was going on around him. Farid was in literature and Ayyoub was in girls.

"You're still in the village, Farid. Up in the mountains!"

Ayyoub made good on his promise and introduced Farid to one of the newly arrived young women. He started seeing her regularly. They'd sit silently together on the high barstools. She couldn't speak or read or write anything besides her mother tongue. He'd order a bottle of cheap Lebanese white wine, or when there weren't any customers he'd order a bottle of Johnny Walker Black. He'd wait for her at closing time to join him at Ayyoub's inn. Farid spent the time hugging her and stroking her hair. He didn't try to kiss her—just held her hands and started teaching her Arabic. "The heart is a bird," and "My grapes are red." And she would repeat after him and hug him back. She refused to take the money he offered her when they parted ways. At the next encounter, she asked him a question Ayyoub had taught her how to say.

"Are you a writer?" she asked, flashing him a sweet smile and following it up with a sentence she memorized from her English lessons. "Write me a love poem!"

And on that evening when Farid got out of the taxi holding a copy of his book and entered "Los Latinos," he found that guy who claimed to be an expert on Arabic grammar and who blinked and winked all the time drinking coffee all alone, so he pulled up a chair and sat with him.

"Is this another book to be proofread?" he asked cautiously.

"No. This book does not require any editing!"

Farid was in a pleasant mood, so he answered his companion's questions about how much money he made and his work hours at the press while they watched music videos playing on the TV screen together, until Luna came out from behind the bar, from the direction of the kitchen. Farid called to her from the distance, waving his long-lost book in the air.

"Luna!" he cried, in clear English. "I have a poem for you…"

Her eyes lit up with joy. He sat beside her, singing along with the song that was filling the place with music, and then finished up with the same enthusiastic tone, addressing the bartender this time. "Wasim, two Jack Daniels!" White wine wasn't going to do the job tonight.

15

The next afternoon, after the evening party when Farid had a few too many shots of American whiskey at Ayyoub's bar, Persephone went downstairs to the press. She stood in the doorway of her husband's office, wearing tight jeans and a white linen top. Her attention shifted from inspecting the shape of her fingernails to gazing deep into the press hallway where the giant Heidelberg machine was sprawled out, as though she were contemplating distant, heavenly horizons.

People said Persephone had broken the rule, being blessed with both beauty and luck. She shined early, at the Debutante Ball that was held at the Ambassadors Hall of Casino du Liban, despite the flashes of light from explosions that could be seen from the balcony in the Beirut sky that Saturday night. It was a spectacular celebration, and out of all the young ladies present, Prince Emmanuel-Philibert de Savoie chose none other than Persephone Melki to waltz with and spend a good portion of the evening talking to.

She became the star among her girlfriends and was well-deserving of the nickname "Sharon Stone" that the math teacher at International College High School gave her one day when she saw Persephone sitting daydreaming at her desk. Everything was said about her that could be said about a girl with such enviable beauty. If a period of time passed without her being seen in the company of a young man, they'd say she liked girls. Or that she was a drug addict if she was seen at parties drinking gin with lime juice to emulate those private investigators in the Raymond Chandler novels she'd started an obsession with. In the summer, she'd get invited to swim at the St. George Hotel pool or for an outing on a speedboat she enjoyed with total abandon. As they set out southward, passing in front of the city of Tyre, she closed her eyes and surrendered to the whipping wind and spraying water, forgetting all about her escort driving the boat who, frankly, was hoping the excursion would lead to something more intimate. Or she would dance into delirium, like she did that famous Saturday night when the star of the Homentmen basketball team with his bulging muscles lifted her up onto his shoulders the moment the ceiling of the night club was opened up, but the pressing crowd knocked her down and she broke her arm, giving the envious girls something to snicker about.

At the age of fourteen her mother began warning her, "Hide your beauty, Perso. When you were a baby, I never let envious eyes catch sight of you. I refused when they wanted to use your picture for a baby formula ad, too. Don't be taken in by nice facades. Look all around yourself. Beirut is full of nice facades."

Her mother, whose beauty she inherited, came to Beirut not knowing a single word of Arabic. She fell in love with the young Lebanese insurance agent her father, the owner of a freighting company, preferred to do business with over the Greek insurance companies. Her mother, whose name her father christened his ship with, giving rise to the saying that George Melki "insured" Theodora Seraphides before marrying her. Whenever "her ship" set anchor in the port of Beirut, sending ripples of joy through the house, she would send Persephone and her brother Salim to the port in bathing suits. They'd board the ship, climbing up the metal ladder. The captain would kiss them and exchange a few greetings in Greek before they vied with each other to hoist the flag atop the mast and bring it back down as if they were playing around in the backyard of their summer home.

Salim inherited the shipping insurance business, dispelling his father's doubts about his ability to handle the responsibilities of the job, based on his behavior and the kind of people he kept company with during his youth which forebode a chaotic future. He expanded the realm of his business and ventured into war insurance. His first big contract was to insure the convoys of food supplies for the American forces in Iraq. And he continued, after the collapse of the state there and in Syria, to take on insurance contracts for trucks of all kinds. He wove a network of relationships that transformed him into a go-to source for getting past dangers. He paid a commission to the Mukhabarat officer at the last Syrian Army checkpoint outside Damascus in the direction of the south, and similarly to the armed resistance in the outskirts of Dara, and more to one of the Bedouin sheikhs who provided a military escort of "goods" upon their exit out of Jordan, crossing with them along with his sons and all their weapons through the length of Anbar Province all the way to the gates of Baghdad. Thus, the Karam family found no one better than Salim Melki to insure the shipment by sea of the Heidelberg machine from Hamburg to the Port of Beirut. They signed a contract with him for it, which, they later expanded to include complete coverage of the entire Press, as well as the house above it, with compensation for theft, destruction, fire, and damages resulting from military operations.

As for the woman of luck and beauty, half of Beirut knew that she and her husband were separated, and the gossipers filled in the details as they wished. They attributed whatever they liked to him and accused her of all sorts of deception and of wanting to get even, cheating with a lover they referred to by name, opening up the entire Karam family history and their printing press, its glory days and the disputes it inherited, the mismanagement and obscure problems, despite which it never shut down, even at night—the evidence of its renewed boom during the past two years. All these were matters that didn't mean much to Persephone, who told her mother not to worry, though unconvincingly, when she called to ask why the police had shown up at the press and what was going to come of it.

Persephone went down to Abdallah's office, passing in front of the workers who humbly lowered their gaze away from their boss's wife—except for the new guy whose secret she held without his knowledge and who she watched in the morning on his way into the press with the look of someone carrying the worries of the world on his shoulders without complaint. He was sure to keep his posture straight as he made his way up the hill from the street to the press. Casting a glance at her window as he reached the entranceway, he'd break off a little branch that he snapped between his fingers or put in his mouth, and plunge his hands into the mass of flowers, plucking a handful of lavender flowers to perfume his jacket pockets with. He took his time entering the press, playing with the tomcats or peeking between the branches of the jacaranda trees at Mount Sanine in the distance, like someone taking encouragement from his native homeland before facing the demands of the day ahead.

That afternoon, she passed through the middle of the big hall and caught his eyes in the distance, twinkling at the knowledge of her presence. She stood in the office doorway, at ease, watching him as he tried to start his copyediting work after lunch. Rarely did he eat in one of the nearby restaurants, preferring to battle his hunger and wait to enjoy his mother's cooking at home. He opens a folder in front of him, shuts it, and opens another. He looks all around, doesn't settle down. He can't work as long as she is standing there. He stands up from his chair and heads toward

Abdallah Karam's office. As he passes by her, she whispers to him in French, "Monsieur Karam isn't here."

The whisper stings him. He gets flustered and answers, "I need to see him about an important matter."

He waits a while.

She moves toward the desk, sits in her husband's place and tries to reach him by phone. First, she tries his cell phone, but it's turned off, so she tries the club he frequents in the afternoons, following in his father's footsteps. Whoever answers the phone asks her his name repeatedly before finally assuring her after a short silence that he hasn't been by today. Two of his friends answer, only to say they don't know where he is. As she talks on the phone, she flashes Farid a smile that is difficult for him to interpret while he waits, excited to be near her, not saying anything for fear of destroying what has started to be woven between them. She finally loses hope of finding Abdallah and heads outside, whispering to him once again, "Don't tell him anything. These matters have nothing to do with him!"

She tried to spark his imagination, but he didn't understand what she said in French in her quick accent. All he got was the warm tone of her voice. He watched how she walked along with her eyes cast down, avoiding eye contact with the employees so as not to be forced to greet them or return their hellos.

When Abdallah Karam came home around seven o'clock in the evening, Persephone asked him where he'd spent the afternoon, under the pretext of being worried about him with all the news of roadblocks and random kidnappings of passersby to exchange for relatives who'd been kidnapped in Syria near Aleppo. He smiled in gratitude for her concern for him and said that as usual he'd been playing cards at the club. She, in her turn, smiled back at him.

16

Farid did not inherit his father's art of seduction. Halim Abu Shaar was a handsome barber about whom his extremely indulgent wife, who remained ever so proud of him even after his death, said that if he'd lived longer, he would have befriended or gotten intimate with every women on Red Cross Street. She told his stories with a lightness that generally did not befit the dead. She knew the details of his private life, which he thought he'd been so adept at keeping secret from her, so well one might think she'd hired a private detective to trail him. But, by an oversight by her and by him, fate drove him in his Renault one day down airport road, when it so happened that the leader of the downtrodden appeared on television and was still in the midst of the introductory prayers, "I take refuge in God from wicked Satan. Praise be to God, the Lord of All Creation, and prayers and peace be upon our master the last of the Prophets, father of al-Qasim, Muhammad son of Abdallah..." when celebratory gunshots were fired in every direction. The barber was hit in the head and bled for half an hour before reaching the hospital, while the roar of the orator was still blaring on his car radio.

He died surrounded by his wife and children who grew up learning early on how to depend on themselves. They left the village, where they had nothing to their name except the house, the best feature of which was the balcony. They returned to the house individually, because its two rooms were no longer big enough to accommodate the numerous children and grandchildren. They came during the summer, and the children would get bored and complain about not having any friends around to play with, so they'd lock up and head back to Beirut. They were three boys. The youngest and mother's favorite was Farid. The two older brothers liked girls and having romantic adventures with them. They were the lone hunter type, never telling a soul about their expeditions. That is, until the three brothers met up one time by a unique coincidence, at a dinner at one of the restaurants known for its diverse mezze. The arak went to their heads and not a single glass was gulped without being clinked by the glasses of the two drinking companions. Tongues were loosened, and soon enough the two brothers started comparing their conquests and sexual prowess. And to attest to their credibility, the two aging teenagers listed the girls one by one, mentioning only the first letter of each one's name. Then the older brother tried to call one on the phone to let his brothers hear her voice, but unfortunately for him, she didn't pick up. The two older brothers didn't leave any room for Farid, in disbelief of the revelations he was hearing from his brothers who were competing with each other and drinking to whoever was paying for the round. The next morning, they felt ashamed and went back to keeping their favorite sport to themselves.

The oldest brother's wife checked her husband's clothes every day. She eavesdropped if he stayed on the phone a long time and tried to follow him if he went out to the balcony to answer. All that to no avail. The second brother's wife was more like her mother-in-law in terms of surrendering to the reality of the situation, but she was capable of blowing up and threatening to leave the house. And that's what happened one time when she found a package of condoms in her husband's pocket, and he claimed not to know the first thing about what they were used for. She went and spent two days with her mother-in-law, but her husband's phone calls saying the children were crying for their mother and that their son, who had been potty trained weeks earlier, started soiling himself again, sent her running back home full of worry and forgetting all about her husband's escapades.

Not much in the way of "literature" found its way to Farid's brothers. They didn't go beyond a high school diploma, and as far as general culture, the few books by Maroun Abboud or Mikhail Naimy whose pages they managed to flip through didn't leave much of an impression on their memories. The expected literary inheritance handed down by the Abu Shaar family fell solely on Farid's shoulders. Despite his not having been close with them, he read their writings like anyone else, and like any familial burden, he tried hard to avoid repeating what they had accomplished in terms of creative styles and genres.

Out of all the Abu Shaar family literati, Farid met only one, the last of his breed. At the age of ten, not long after his father died, Farid's mother took him to visit him one rainy day. She'd woken him up early, got him all washed up and dressed him in his Sunday best. He wore his winter shoes with all the perforations and the long laces. She wore her only overcoat, the red one, and pinned on her golden cat brooch. From time to time, in the two taxis that transported them in succession all the way to Bliss Street near the American University, she would cast him a look of dismay as she adjusted his collar or patted down a stray strand of his hair.

They entered a quiet building whose entryway and staircase were carpeted. Not a sound could be heard except the old elevator making its ascent and then clanging to a stop at one of the floors. As the maid escorted them to the parlor, she whispered to them that she would not interrupt "the Professor's" reading, but he would not be kept away in the library too long, for she knew his routine. His mother did not remove her overcoat despite the warm temperature. She sat Farid down next to her and began whispering to him. She was trembling, too, and pulled him close to her whenever he moved the slightest bit away from her, as if she didn't want the two of them to take up more than one person's seat on the sofa. Finally, out came the man who had been described in a magazine article once as being of "average height, full physique, olive complexion, stately, highly astute though humble, unhurried in his speech, not given to laughter, chaste of tongue, quick to understand, strong of memory, venerable, affable, and when he spoke, captivated hearts." He was wearing a brocaded *abaya* and had a lightweight skullcap on his head made of white yarn. Farid's mother nudged him to stand up and greet him with her. The entire time he spoke with Farid's mother, the man nicknamed Yusuf "the Erudite" Abu Shaar rested one hand on Farid's head, while holding his mother's hand with the other as he asked about her health and how the children were faring. Then he asked Farid to join him in the library. The mother stood back, watching her little man clasping the hand of his relative who let him go in first before shutting the door behind them.

Despite the rain, some bright beams of sunshine crept in between the drapes over the high windows, illuminating the shelves of books with the golden titles imprinted on their covers. Their bright light blinded Farid's eyes as he entered, preventing him at first from seeing the shelves filled from floor to ceiling with black and red books, which he imagined ever since that day as having colorful sleeping dwarfs and dancing genies living inside them.

Their seclusion didn't last long. Fifteen minutes later Yusuf the Erudite opened the door and called to Farid's mother, who told her son to sit and wait for her on the sofa. The boy remembered that his mother's isolation in that room lasted a long time and that she came out with red cheeks, Yusuf following behind with an envelope he was licking shut. He handed her the envelope and bid them farewell at the door with a loving smile. The boy asked his mother what was in the envelope. She ignored him, so he asked again. Still she said nothing. He put the ball back in her court again, but she didn't return the volley.

Sitting in the taxi, it was his mother's turn now to ask Farid what transpired between the two of them. He did not reciprocate her unwillingness to spill the secret, telling her all about how when they entered the library, Yusuf Abu Shaar started searching for a book while reciting a line of poetry:

My longing brought your face before me in al-Zahraa'
The horizon unfurled itself and the view of the earth was pure delight

Farid responded by continuing:

And the ailing breeze wafted before sunset
As if taking pity on me it fell ill with sympathy

He told her of Yusuf's amazement and how he stopped searching for the book and instead asked Farid if he understood the meaning of "the ailing breeze" and the reason for its "taking pity." Farid answered correctly, leaving his relative to stare at him in disbelief. Farid's mother hugged him and kissed him on his forehead. Unable to contain her pride for her son, as though it was a manifestation of her excellent childrearing, she whispered in his ear, "You're just like your father. The ladies are going to love you, too!"

But she didn't tell him that the money in the envelope that Yusuf Abu Shaar had given her was to pay for Farid's tuition, and that it was the second time he'd given her money since her husband's death. This time, though, he had wished to meet the boy. Now that he had seen the boy's giftedness himself, he promised to continue supporting him as long as he lived. When he died, Farid had reached his final years of school. He composed an elegy for him and delivered it at his funeral. The president of the American University attended, as did several AUB faculty members. And there at Christ Bible Baptist Church, the son of Halim Abu Shaar realized that his so-called kinsman had been an Evangelical, and not a Maronite like them.

17

The truth was, Abdelhamid al-Halwany was not the docile type. He spent his life switching from one press to another. The day he was fired from the American Press, he asked the press director Reverend Timothy Harris permission to take his "personal belongings" with him. He brought a white linen sack and filled it with five complete sets of embellished letters in initial form, from *alif* to *yaa'*, and along with it an assortment of *Bismallahs* in different fonts and a variety of flourishes and various embellishments for the page margins, too. He hired a porter, strapped three heavy wooden boxes to his back, and led the way to his house. His wife found a nice empty space in the kitchen, to the right of the sink, where they stacked up the boxes. Then she busied herself arranging all sorts of jars and containers on top of them—jams and spices and salt and the little pine seedlings growing in clay pots. Abdelhamid shoved the bag under his bed with his foot, where it would be out of sight. For decades, no one took any interest in knowing what was inside those wooden boxes, and likewise, Abdelhamid did not take them with him to the press run by the Jesuits, who were always vying to hire him whenever he and Fuad Karam had a falling out.

Abdelhamid's heart didn't hold out long. He died sitting in a chair, before having a chance to remove the tarbush from his head, after suffering a violent coughing fit as he set the type for the new edition of the Mass book. It had two columns on each page—Syriac in red to the right and the Arabic translation in black to the left—per request of the Maronite bishop of Beirut, Augustinos Mubarak. Mustapha al-Halwany inherited the house, and the sealed boxes remained a part of the family's kitchen furniture, until one day no less than eighty years later when the grandson Anis noticed they were there. That was at the time when the Karam family converted the last cellar of the horse stables building into a museum for all the tools of the trade that they had inherited over the years. He brought them over by taxi, as a kind of token to his grandfather, and added them into the Karam's collection of printing machines and traditional tools. They remained there all boxed up for years, until one day when a worker accidentally knocked one down, causing it to spill out onto the floor. Anis spent two full days inspecting the contents of the boxes, imagining his grandfather Abdelhamid's madness to have produced so early on what many had given up trying to produce in a later period. He had engraved and molded a complete set, with all the embellishments and extras, of *Thuluth* script, the king of Arabic calligraphic fonts and most splendid and unrivalled.

Anis assembled it and then forgot all about it once again. He didn't remember it until one day when Fleur came calling after him down at the press, "Monsieur Anis," pointing up at the second floor. Mrs. Persephone was sitting waiting for him amid all those books of hers open face down around her. She was holding the red notebook, turning its pages without focus and without stopping.

She addressed him directly, getting straight to the point.

"Will you print one copy of this book for me?"

Master Anis knew she had difficulty reading Arabic.

"It's for a friend of mine. It's her dream to have it published. I want to give it to her as a birthday present."

Master Anis immediately recognized Farid Abu Shaar's notebook, but he pretended to believe her. He'd made it a habit to go along with behavior he didn't understand, and he was also not interested in saying no to Persephone, who was challenging him to make it the very best printing job he could do.

Then she threw out a surprising question. "Do you come to the press at night, Anis?"

He pretended not to hear her, trying to gain some time, but she repeated the question. He asked her to clarify, under the pretense of not understanding her broken Arabic. When he asked what she meant by "night," she answered, "Midnight," to which he spontaneously replied in the negative. He inquired about the reason for her question, and when he suddenly realized why, he conceded to coming once or twice a month when printing jobs got backed up and deadlines had to be met.

She requested he use the most expensive paper he could find in Beirut and that he do the typesetting by hand. She wanted him to run it on the old press, by hand, too, if possible. She wanted it to be a handcrafted work of art.

"I hate those modern machines. They scare me!"

Lutfi Karam scared her, too.

She impressed upon Anis not to tell anyone, so as not to ruin her friend's surprise. For the first time ever, she asked him to keep it secret from her husband.

"Don't tell Dudul!"

Anis stood there staring at her, not knowing what to say, when she suddenly asked him an even more uncomfortable question.

"Do you stay down there all by yourself at night?"

Anis got tongue-tied once again, shrugging his shoulders as he feigned not to know what she meant and hurried off before Persephone could ask any more questions. He wondered what would make a woman like her show the least bit of concern for that gloomy-faced copyeditor. He was forced to retrace his steps to make sure he understood.

"Did you say one copy, Madame?"

"Yes, just one."

She pointed to a painting by George Cyr, who had been a friend of her great-grandfather and painted depictions of the Gulf of Beirut—the port, the city, and the mountains in the background drowning in a pink fog reminiscent of the gradations of color she had chosen for the wall paint in her house.

"Just like this painting. There is no other like it…"

Despite Persephone's befuddling questions, the project had awakened a desire in him that had been buried under years of idleness.

She returned to her bedroom and he went out, shutting the door behind him and forgetting himself as he stood beside the statue of Venus with her head turned trying to peek at her own naked bottom while his head was bent down to peruse the pages he held in his hands as he began planning how to dazzle Persephone with the retrieval of his long-lost printing skills.

⁂

He spent days in the cellar where the old tools were stored, hunched over his work. He knew it would most likely be the last time he would ever get the opportunity to set type and produce a book all on his own. The moment he reached for the box of metal letters, the scent of his father Mustapha came back to him. It stuck to him in his youth from constant contact with him on his comings and goings. His father had taken him out of school early, under the pretext of his profession not requiring him to know how to read, beyond being able to decipher the individual letters. He took him out early and trained him in the art of printing, the only form of capital he could hand down to his son.

It was unknown how Anis was able to convince Abdallah Karam to give him so much time off. He only summoned him when there was a task no one else could do as well as he could. When he passed by the other workers, they noticed a bright sparkle in his eye they'd never seen before. He would hurry back to get started arranging his grandfather Abdelhamid's letters in a wooden tray, before arranging the pages in quartos, each of which held eight pages. He had twenty eight-page sections to arrange ahead of him. He lost himself as he lined up the pieces, paying careful attention to the succession of the letters and the flow of the connectors. He didn't glean any meaning from the words and sentences, or was not interested in the meanings anyway. Lutfi Karam was seen more than once heading toward the back cellar while Anis was holed up there all day, not leaving for home until a very late hour. His wife called once, as evening fell, worried he might have gotten hurt somehow or kidnapped, because she had been talking on the phone with the press owner's secretary who was relating to her what she was observing with her own eyes right then and there from her balcony: crowds of Sunni and Shiite youths facing off against each other in the neighborhood— one group at the top of the street insulting Ali and Zeinab, and another gang on the opposite side cursing Othman and Omar, calling to avenge al-Husein.[7] They threw whatever they could get their hands on at each other, which eventually lead to their firing missiles at each other as had often happened before, killing and injuring many.

Anis assembled the pages with care, secured them, and turned on the same ancient printing press his father, and possibly his grandfather, too, had operated and which had been converted to work on electric power at some point. It started up again for the first time in more than fifty years and turned out an initial page proof on regular paper, which allowed him to attend to adjusting and rearranging things in accordance with the proper *Thuluth* measurements. He would find little errors. Tiny idiosyncrasies that would go unnoticed by the general reader would catch his attention, so he'd mark them in red. The work distracted him from any coherent reading. He took it apart, fine-tuned it, and secured it once again.

All that remained was to choose the paper, and he knew exactly what was demanded of him. He got permission from Lutfi Karam and headed to his cellar. He slid the two moveable stones away from the wall and there appeared the hidden cubby hole. He took the small amount of paper he needed from inside, tossed the copyeditor's red notebook in, and locked the precious cache back up. He cut the pages and turned the machine on for the last time. Out came the final, revised, clean copy. He picked it up and carried it outside to see it in the daylight. He was delighted by what he saw. He had chosen a fancy binding for it and was himself astounded he hadn't thought to print even one additional copy of the book, at the very least.

18

The Karam Brothers' crown jewel—or what was said to be the most modern printing press in all the Middle East, which was tantamount to a two-story structure resembling a warship that required a ladder for the workers to get on top of, and which required a crew of at least six men to attend to its maintenance and effusive output—this crown jewel did not dock in the Port of Beirut inside a custom-sized container as easily as one might expect. Securing the funds was a grueling sequence of negotiations with bank managers that lasted over a year, and which nearly collapsed on many an occasion on account of outstanding debts owed by Karam Brothers, despite revisions to the payment schedule made possible by political favors. They were permitted one final grace period, per a decision by the bank board of trustees made after the terrible assassination incident and the horrible injury suffered by Abdallah Karam as he exited the bank's main branch.

The requested sum—several million U.S. dollars—was not granted until the owners of the press made personal guarantees and put up collateral: they mortgaged all their personal property, in addition to the entire contents of the press, the trade name, the building—including the living quarters on the second floor, the shares they acquired in Solidere, in exchange for textile shops they'd owned in the old souks, and Abdallah's maternal uncle's horse farm in the Beqaa Valley. In short, the Heidelberg Speedmaster XL 162 gobbled up the entire inheritance of

Madame Evelyn, whose biography had been published in French by a Lebanese journalist. The biography included an appendix of personal correspondences that she exchanged with Charles Corm, George Schehadé, and Marguerite Yourcenar.[8] Madame Evelyn was Abdallah's grandmother—the only child to one of the wealthiest well-known Beiruti families, and whose father had been bestowed with the title of viscount by His Holiness the Pope. That same woman who never missed an opportunity to recount stories of Jamal Basha bouncing her on his knees at the tender age of two, when he would come to the house at the invitation of her parents for dinner and dancing during the Great War. But the thing no one ever mentioned in front of her, was that her mother had been one of the many lovers—whose names were on everyone's lips— of this member of the triumvirate leadership of the Turkish Party of Union and Progress.

The colossal investment was undertaken at a time when the Syndicate of Press Owners, whose council sessions Lutfi Karam had been absent from ever since his son Abdallah's injury, never tired during their monthly meetings of tallying up the orders that had been cancelled in the sector, and the deals that got postponed despite being only a handshake away from concluding. They parleyed back and forth about the ever-growing number of kidnappings for political gain or ransom money. They deplored the cessation of the new school program that a committee under American supervision was putting in place in Iraq, which would have distributed contracts for the millions of copies of textbooks they would need to several Lebanese presses. They also bemoaned the withdrawal of a huge contract with the United Arab Emirates, who had ordered a series of Prophetic Hadiths for free distribution to Islamic organizations and bookstores around the world; they'd opted instead to make it available for free download on the internet. What was worse, that idea had come from a former Beirut printer who'd gone into digital publishing. Then their conversation would stray to other topics. They'd disagree on the number of refugees fleeing from the war in Syria, or they'd ruminate about the demonstrations protesting caricatures of the Prophet Muhammad and how people smashed shops and threatened to set fire to the downtown commercial area and bring in poor people from the outskirts of the city to stand in the fancy storefronts right in the heart of the capital. And there was that owner of one of the biggest advertising companies who died, leaving behind a widow who wished to close the business, which undoubtedly would lead to the collapse of the high-class magazines that were funded by ads for perfume, famous-label lingerie, and expensive writing instruments. The last thing said by the owner of Al-Anwar Press upon concluding the handshake on the Karam family's deal to buy the Heidelberg, who spoke in a perfect British accent he'd attained through years of studying at the London School of Economics (borrowing from the warning written on the rearview mirrors of American cars) was, "Things in the mirror might be 'worse' than they appear." His comments were attributed to jealousy, and the subject was closed.

Matters certainly were ambiguous. The general situation was deteriorating, and Abdallah Karam and those behind him, like his echo, Master Anis al-Halwany, grumbled about everything—from public bids to meddling with the books to favor warlords new to power and influence who had gained seats in parliament, to the revolutions that had undermined the markets of neighboring Arab countries without which Beirut could not survive, to the rise in price of paper and how some "protégés" had managed to import it without paying customs fees. The heir of Karam Brothers Press would be singing this sad tune of his out of allegiance to a tradition by which merchants in the capital could advance and rake in profits, lamenting the loss of a golden age they'd heard so much talk about, that their fathers lived through, so they said. But the people who lived through it remembered how those same fathers of theirs had filled the world with lamentations in their day, too. It was as though, in this city, complaining was the key to success.

The situation was deteriorating, as the economists and journalists confirmed. But Karam Brothers' printing press was running at full speed. The Karam family's amazing machine surpassed all their hopes. The monthly bank payments were being made in full, the arrears owed to the National Social Security Fund were paid off, and they were meeting payroll on the last day of every month. The accountant of Karam Brothers Press, who had been with the company for over twenty-five years, noticed a huge influx of printing contracts that were massive not only in terms of numbers but also in the extent of their strange nature. There was one for a series of fancy illustrated art books about the Mayan and Aztec civilizations, and another for hundreds of thousands of high-quality, heavy paper shopping bags stamped with the logo for Lanvin or Adidas, placed by companies with headquarters in Macau or the British Virgin Islands. After asking the men running the Heidelberg machine a few off-the-cuff questions, the accountant was able to verify that the work was in full swing, but he didn't let himself be too curious so as not to have it backfire on him, and also in deference to his father's adage, "Stay away from evil and sing it a happy song!" He contented himself to tend to whatever documents and receipts reached his desk. He categorized them and prepared a balance sheet listing all the expenses, including a sizeable cushion of emergency funds, and still the figures representing surplus and profit were unprecedented. Not seeing any reason to deprive himself from benefitting from the unexpected boon, he decided to ask for a raise, which, as he expected, was agreed to without question.

Persephone didn't need to see the accounting books to notice the huge improvements underway all around her. She saw the start of renovations to the building that had been postponed since first moving the press there, and the road coming up from the main street was being paved and streetlights were being installed. She overheard Abdallah saying something about opening a bank account in Geneva, in Swiss francs. Twice he traveled to Paris on business, the nature of which was a mystery to Persephone.

She got on the phone in the morning.

"The money has been streaming in for months, Mom. I don't know where from. I don't feel good about it. I see ghosts down in the press and hear voices. And they hired a new night watchman who makes me uncomfortable."

Theodora Seraphides didn't know if her daughter really believed what she was saying. Meanwhile, Persephone went on to comment derisively about her mother-in-law having arrived one day as if on some urgent and momentous mission. She reached into her purse and pulled out a huge eye amulet made of genuine turquoise from Iran. She hung it above the doorway of the press, to ward of the evil eye.

"I'm like a cat or a dog. I sense danger before it arrives!"

Her mother worried about her and those fantasies of hers. She told her to say her prayers every night before going to sleep, knowing she wouldn't listen. Either that or she held her father responsible for filling her head with all those detective stories.

"You took the entire Black Series home with you, didn't you?"

"And I make sure to buy every new one that comes out…"

Persephone completes her morning round of phone calls by calling her friend. She talks about the tall young man who came to the press one day with a notebook.

"Do you remember Noubar, Sarah? He talks like Noubar. He stood there like a soldier on alert in front of Dudul in his office and said he had poured his soul into that notebook, like someone saying he poured some pistachios into a paper bag. Noubar was like that, too. He was never satisfied with his dancing until he felt he'd poured his soul into it."

"Where do you find these guys, Perso?" Sarah asked, before switching to other subjects. "Or do you make them up?"

19

Business at the press was booming, and Abdallah was also beginning to regain his strength. He started out taking slow, sluggish walks that became more stable and in time developed into light Saturday morning jogs along Corniche al-Manara with his driver. He wore a cap to hide the bald spot on his head until the hair grew back. He regained his appetite, too, and craved *knafeh bil-jibn* and *mughrabiyyeh* with lamb shanks, which he'd tasted at the home of one of his Muslim friends. He went back to smoking Super Partagas cigars with a glass of chilled port on pleasant evenings while patting Gogol, the Bichon Maltese, who Fleur shooed away from Sabine and Nicole as they drifted off to sleep.

And another transformation took place within him: an urgent desire for the female body that overwhelmed his senses. Unlike usual, he would wake up in the middle of the night, hot with desire, or maybe it was the desire that woke him up. The female employees at the press who came into his office noticed this change in him after he returned to work still wearing the robe of Saint Anthony the Great. They started feeling uncomfortable around him, not knowing quite how to sit with him ogling them like that. He checked out their bottoms, gazed at their bare shoulders, tawny skin, and their cleavage. Their fingers turned him on. His brash scrutinizing started with the hands. He'd take a break from press matters and spend his time between betting on ball games or playing Texas Hold'Em and searching for photos of nude women, or partially nude, standing or sitting in provocative poses. He'd enlarge the photo on the screen, crop it until nothing was left except a pair of thighs with no face, or two open lips he'd enlarge some more and gaze at passionately.

That did not satisfy Abdallah, though. He wanted the full, real experience. So, he called a friend of his, known to be an expert on such matters, asking for his "services," which the man was happy to oblige. To fulfill his request, and because the world was small, and Beirut was even smaller, this friend turned to none other than the owner of Los Latinos to be Abdallah's escort into the world of women. He urged him to find the most spirited one in bed, so Ayyoub directed him to the brunette with the green eyes who introduced herself as having a Moroccan father and an Iranian mother. Ayyoub knew that customers there would pay double for a girl of their own race. Indeed, he had come up with a convincing theory having to do with incest.

If Abdallah's middle-man friend heard anyone suggesting that the owner of Karam Brothers Press had become impotent after being injured in the explosion, he'd respond by saying, "The thing one should fear most is a calm sea." He paid his tab for him and gave Ayyoub a check to pay for the girl. He wanted to treat Abdallah to it, without him having to give anything in return—if only for this first time at least, a small gift to a friend for having recovered from his injuries.

Abdallah was asked not to wait in the lobby of the hotel overlooking the sea, but to go straight to the room where the girl would meet him a few minutes later. It took only a few minutes of touching her for Abdallah to reach orgasm. She appeased him in a heavy Egyptian accent that completely contradicted what he'd been told about her origins, and it occurred to him that they might have sent him a different girl than the one they'd promised. She told him not to worry; this kind of thing happened to a lot of men. Abdallah got up, went to the bathroom to wash, and then came back with renewed determination. This time, he lasted a good long time. Ayyoub confided to his friend that whenever that girl talked about Abdallah she would burst out laughing. "That short fat guy is more virile than all of you!" She'd say. "He doesn't need a thing to get him going." She also said that if ever she wanted to do some dallying "on the side," out of all her customers, he'd be her first choice.

But the way the man with the deep scar on his face behaved with the girls, while his driver waited for him outside the door to the hotel the whole time he was up on the thirteenth floor, was entirely unexpected. As soon as he started having frequent trysts with the girl of many nationalities and accents, and she got familiar with him and started telling him her life story—how she'd appeared on a TV talent show at one time and got invited after that by a talent agent to come to Beirut and sing at the New Year's Eve celebration. She got a lot of attention and an offer to stay on, in a furnished apartment, for an amount of money she couldn't refuse. She sent some of her earnings to her mother who was suffering from bilharzia, and some to her little brother. As soon as she started that, Abdallah started looking for another girl. Discovering that his bed partner was an ordinary woman who complained of being sick or needing something or even about her monthly menstruation, was a sure-fire way to weaken his desire for her. He wanted his lover to be perfect, to have a body with no weaknesses, no bodily functions other than providing pleasure and bliss. She should be clean, always ready, and well-kept. And handing the girl money directly for her services as she left the room—a little ahead of him for camouflage— didn't bother him a bit. He preferred to pay them directly. To him, the girl's desire for the money was what sparked his desire for her. The more practice he got with his new hobby, the more particular his requests became. Ayyoub was bewildered as to how to satisfy this lavish customer of his, indeed the most lavish of all. He knew who he was but pretended he didn't. His requests were very specific and came to Ayyoub via text messages from Abdallah's middle-man friend. One time he wanted a girl who didn't speak any of the languages commonly spoken in Beirut—Arabic, French, or English. Ayyoub thought he wanted it that way so she would keep his secret safe. Other times, he couldn't figure out why he asked for her to be wearing fishnet stockings, or wanted one over thirty, or a black one from Africa, if available.

Abdallah Karam stayed away from anything that reminded him of his wife: blue eyes, short blond hair, soft white skin. He had never asked her about her previous romances, but he did notice her behavior, like at a class reunion dinner once when she clinked glasses time after time with an old classmate of his and then went over to whisper something in his ear before they both burst out laughing, or at the Scrabble competition where he noticed how she chose to sit next to the only other man participating in the competition, and at the press with that young copyeditor who followed her every move and with whom she wasn't stingy about exchanging glances. When his secretary told him that the copyeditor was asking for him, he called Farid Abu Shaar to his office and asked him what he wanted. And so, Farid improvised a description of what he had in mind ever since his manuscript had gone missing one night only to reappear on another night in published form.

"The telephone book I'm working on editing now is quite big and heavy—hundreds and hundreds of pages—and I can't carry it home to work on. Would you allow me to stay here at the press after hours, so I can work on it?"

He agreed without further discussion. He didn't know anything about this young man he'd hired so hastily, so he delved into a long conversation with him—was he married or single, where was he born, where did he live? Farid's answers were curt. Then Abdallah remembered that when the young man came to the press for the first time, he'd had some sort of manuscript or notebook with him that he was hoping to publish, and so he asked him a probing question: "What are you writing these days?"

"I'm writing..." he said and then couldn't think of anything to add and so he corrected himself as if speaking to himself. "No, no. Nothing. I stopped writing."

Abdallah didn't back down. He wanted to find out for sure whether this Arabic copyeditor was an idiot or level-headed, so he went on asking him questions about this and that just to keep him talking.

"Do you have a university degree?"

"I don't believe in academic degrees, but I do have a certificate in languages for which I did a comparative study between Abdalqaaher al-Jurjani's *Dala'il al-i'jaaz* (Proofs of Inimitability) and Ferdinand de Saussure's *Course in General Linguistics*."

Abdallah had opened a door to things he didn't know much about, so he reverted to asking more general questions.

"When did you used to write? Where did you used to write?"

20

Farid Abu Shaar wrote standing up. He'd heard once that standing keeps you alert, so up he stood. He didn't write wearily, but with all his senses ignited. He liked to imagine himself burning like a flame as he wrote, always with his favorite fountain pen—the silver Montblanc he inherited from his father, who in his time had received it as a gift from his relative Suleiman Abu Shaar to encourage him, when, in his youth, he had shown a fleeting curiosity for books and writers. But Farid's father dreamed of a different world and never took the expensive pen out of its case except the day of his wedding so he, his bride, and their witnesses could sign the church registry, and another time to sign the IOUs—with prepaid interest—he took out from loan sharks when he had no other choice and needed money to open up his salon, *Chez Halim*, in Furn al-Shubbak, and furnish it with two circular barber's chairs and large mirrors. Halim died young and left the pen to his youngest son.

Farid was in fourth grade when he composed his first original lines. It was in Arabic class, prompted by one of the Arabic teacher's favorite assignments—"Compose a sentence using this word." On that day, he started them with the word "apple." The goal was for the children to build a "subject," "verb," and "direct object" around this common fruit, and come up with a simple sentence such as, "The boy ate the apple." Maybe the advanced ones among them would make a longer one, like, "Adam left Eden because he ate the apple."

And so, it was quite the surprise to him and to his classmates when Farid stood up and said in a poetic tone:

"The earth is a red apple that moves along gingerly."

The teacher raised his hand, signaling the class to be silent, as though not to taint the miraculous event that had just taken place there in the classroom. He then proceeded to ask the boy how old he was, if he'd had private tutoring, and so on. When Farid's answers eventually revealed his family name, the teacher shook his head and let out a great sigh of relief for having found in the boy's relation to the Abu Shaar family a genetic basis for his proficiency with the Arabic language and his poetic precociousness.

Farid did his writing up in his village where, while deep in thought searching for expression, the sounds of cannon fire reached him from beyond the chain of mountains—a battle in the Syrian interior raged at night and the dead were left strewn in the open for days, as was broadcast in the news media the next day. He wrote standing up, with his papers and pen resting on the village church lectern that the priest agreed to let him borrow throughout the summer, except on Sundays. It was the same stand on which they placed the Holy Gospel, or the Synaxarion—the book of the lives of the saints, left open even when there wasn't a reader standing before it. Farid would take it out onto the balcony and stand behind it, facing the little juniper forest on the mountainside. Sometimes he could hear the sounds of scattered gunfire from hunting rifles when a flock of migratory quail or pheasants would alight there. He went specifically to the village for that purpose, devoting two or three days to writing—in the morning before breakfast and in the evening until the light of day forsook him. He came there when he failed to find a publisher for his book and the only offer he got was a job as a copyeditor.

He stood before the juniper forest with the Temple of Bacchus in the distance, and for the sake of regaining some self-confidence he recited passages from his own writings into the open space in a loud voice that set some dogs in the area barking. Farid recalled as part of his emotional self-therapy how his grandfather had sat him on his lap one day, on this same balcony that was drenched in a sea of gardenias as he remembered from his childhood. He bounced him on his knees and exclaimed that the world only "produces" a genius once every hundred years. It produced Khalil Gibran at the turn of the twentieth century, and "Soon this boy's turn will come around."

He wrote in blue ink, never letting go of the Montblanc. He refilled the ink twice a day. He felt the pen contained traces of those who had written with it before him, and despite the extent to which he insisted on his individuality and the uniqueness of his style and didn't owe anything to anyone, he was attached to that pen that many Abu Shaar hands had held before him. He kept a sizeable supply of "Parker" ink cartridges, which were no longer widely available in bookstores, and two extra nibs for the tip he happened to find by chance. He wrote with beautiful, slanted penmanship, going easy on the tip for upward strokes and heavy for downward strokes. Whenever his young nephews happened to be in the village, they liked to spy on him and snicker at him, watching how he used the ink blotter to dab each line several times after writing it. He never crossed anything out. He waited for the words to come to him. He sifted them and selected them carefully, repeating the sentence in his mind over and over, and then closed his eyes, sinking into the depths of his soul. He'd say it aloud before writing it down very slowly and with discipline. He avoided making mistakes as much as possible, but if he did make one or if some stray drops of ink ran from the Montblanc onto the paper, he'd tear it up and write it all over again.

He wrote standing up, and he read standing up, too. He read Sheikh Ibrahim al-Yazigi's translation of the Holy Bible from

Genesis to Revelations. He was bent on devouring everything Yusuf Abu Shaar—the man who'd paid all his tuition expenses—sent to him before he died: a box full of books he'd owned more than one copy of, which was delivered to him by the husband of the woman who served him as housekeeper his entire life. Al-Jahiz's *Al-Mahaasin wa-l-addaad* (The Book of Virtues and their Opposites), the book *Akhbaar al-A'yaan fi jabal Lubnaan* (Chronicles of the Notables of Mount Lebanon) by Tannous al-Chidiaq, and when he placed before him on the lectern *Kitaab al-Mawaqif wa yaliihi kitaab al-mukhatabaat* (The Mawaqif and the Mukhatabat) by Muhammad Bin Abd al-Jabbaar Bin Hasan al-Niffari and read in the preface, "[This book] captures the opening up of the self onto the pure, internal existence that it has stored up since all eternity; it unveils the hidden things of the self and of existence and their many worlds, revealing them before the self itself," this 'pure, eternal, inner self' filled him with delight. He was eager to read. He opened to a random page.

> God says to his servant, 'I created you in my image as an individual who can hear and see and speak. I made you for the glorification of my names and to be the object of my care. You are my vision with no curtain between you and me. You are my companion and there is no border between you and me. Oh servant, there is no distance separating you from me. You are closer to me than to yourself. I am closer to you than your own speech...'

He felt an urgent need to write without having a specific idea in mind. An undeniable desire took hold of him, and he felt as if he were filled and brimming over. He felt as though the words were stored up inside him, had been born with him or existed before he came into being, eternally. He only had to wait to finally encounter them and all he had to do was be open to these words and not betray them. To be patient only until they emerged to the surface through a labor that was difficult at times. Bouts of inspiration would hit him at night. He'd sit up in bed and reach for an available pen and write on anything he could—a paper napkin or on the palm of his hand if he couldn't find something else, in the dark of his bedroom. He wrote down whichever expression that was imposing itself on him and keeping him awake on anything he could find so that in the light of day he could write it down in finished form.

He reached the end when the bouts of writing diminished. He poured out everything he had, as if having delivered his message he could rest. He began reviewing what he had written, reading aloud to make sure the rhythm of the sentences was just right. He adjusted their rises and falls, pausing a long time between two consecutive adjectives. He allowed himself to start some sentences with the subject rather than the verb, composing nominal sentences and using one-word expressions, before revising and revising the ending until he achieved a rhythm that delighted him. He assembled the papers he'd written in the form of a notebook and bound them with a red cover. He carried it with him to Beirut and showed it to all the publishing houses, one by one, after finding directions to each one in the guide put out by the Printers and Publishers Union, which was established in 1934. He started putting his red notebook on the little night table next to his bed at night and never left home without tucking it under his arm, until what happened happened.

But one disturbing night after returning from Los Latinos, and having drunk more than usual, Farid saw himself in a dream heading to the village alone. In the dream, he gathers some dry juniper branches and builds a fire like the one he used to dance around on the Feast of Transfiguration with his little friends in the village. He throws his red book into the fire and waits for it to turn to ashes. He is relieved of it, as if he'd never written it, as if it never existed. He burns it and hears a familiar voice say to him,

"I swear by God, I did not burn you until I was almost burned by you!"[9]

But when he woke up the next morning, he was calm, with nothing left of his dream but an obscure memory.

21

They came in the middle of the day this time, before the lunch break—three new agents from the Anti-Financial Crimes Division. One was a young woman dressed in a specked military uniform, the only one carrying a weapon in plain view—a Glock 17 pistol at her hip; the other two were men, dressed in unstylish civilian clothing. All three of them were of small build. At least, that's how they appeared to anyone who saw them come through the door to Karam Brothers Press next to the brawny, blond-haired man they were escorting. He was a foreigner sent by Interpol from its main headquarters in Lyon, France, and carrying with him some twenty-euro notes with their predominantly blue hue, issued by the State of Finland and with an architectural sketch on the back reminiscent of the windows of cathedrals of the Middle Ages, like others depicting doors or bridges, symbols of openness and cooperation among peoples.

That long chapter had begun far away, beyond the seas, the day two undercover agents from the Brazilian Anti-Riot and Anti-Narcotics Force arrested in the slums of Rio de Janeiro on the outskirts of "Cidade de Deus," one Jesus Gilberto, aka "Anaconda," born in Montevideo. At the station they beat him hard, as was their norm, especially after they discovered the large number of arrest warrants issued on him. Apart from trafficking cocaine—not insignificant quantities of which were confiscated from a pouch under his motorcycle seat—he confessed to smuggling money into

Brazil via the land border with Uruguay. The intelligence services came right away, pouncing on the chance to investigate the other big fish in the area he helped them reel in. The whole matter was concluded with a sort of a handshake with the public prosecutor after the detainees explained how the "goods" came in from Gambia, along the Atlantic coast, packed inside doors and engines of used Mercedes that reached them via one of the historical slave trade routes to Latin America. The police in Montevideo knew that once the smugglers received the money, they could deposit it in banks with the help of bribed employees, or through small money changers who, with a little time, could plant it inside bundles of cash and send it back to Europe or other places around the world. In Banjul, a quiet, forgotten town on the opposite coast of the Atlantic, it turned out the merchandise made its way to the airport quite normally, in luggage checked on by legitimate passengers that no one bothered. Their suitcases were put into the plane's storage hold during the flight and were returned to the passengers when they landed. The investigation went on for months. The officers at the regional Interpol center in Argentina put together a comprehensive relief map covering four continents, along with a list of names of those in custody and those still at large. And they pinned little colored flags marking the cities where this network was known to operate, and they also made a film of the map in three dimensions. And then one day, they finally arrived at the magical name of the source from where it all originated: Beirut.

Meanwhile, at 20 Sonnemaanstrasse Street in Frankfurt, the currency printing experts from the European Central Bank applied themselves to their favorite sport: feeling the paper and checking for the rough surface, sharp edges, and the squeaking sound made when rubbed with the hand. The magnetic strip functioned, allowing the bills to pass easily through counting machines. And when they passed it under the light, they were able to see the watermark of Europa, the heroine of Greek mythology who, it was said, was abducted by Zeus. Appearing to her in the form of a handsome white bull, he enticed the young maiden to mount him, and off he rode with her from the shores of Tyre. The security thread was there, and the front and back were nearly perfectly aligned. The feel and look of the bills were an amazing feat. Their only weakness: the colors didn't change when tilted under the light, and they were lacking the microprint that can only be seen under a microscope. These "Finnish" specimens amazed the experts, having incorporated nearly all of the fifteen security features. As they wrote in their report, they were convinced that whoever had made the bills most certainly did so using the latest generation of modern digital printers, of either German or Swiss manufacture, to be exact.

That was enough to narrow down the possibilities to a few addresses in Beirut, which were raided in the early morning hours at roughly the same time. They impounded a number of articles and specimens, but despite the show of force and their occupation of the printing presses for half a day, they were not able to put their hands on any useful evidence. This is what was imparted to Abdallah Karam the afternoon of the first raid, so he decided not to worry and said openly to any of his friends who asked, that the press was "protected," insinuating that some powerful political, or possibly military, force had the press's back. The one bit of news about what was taking place that appeared in the news media was a blurb buried in the inner pages of *Al-Bilad* (The Nation) newspaper, which was known for its sensational news stories. It reported that an "international" investigation was underway that might implicate a "long-established" institution for its involvement in "illegal activities." The Lebanese information systems expert, who had just returned from a cyber-crimes internship in London, was content to get into the computer files, where he found printing contracts and pictures of naked women. He even stumbled upon a file of brief diary entries written by one of the employees. Some of what was written caught his attention—inequity in the treatment of men and women at the press, where the favoritism was being shown toward the women, and one writer's observation:

> "Something is going on at the press at night. I can tell because I am usually the last one to leave at the end of the day, and when I return in the morning, little things have changed. No one would notice them, but I am sure of it."

The expert was also able to read the majority of emails exchanged through Outlook Express, one of which caught his attention containing a description of how beautiful the press owner's wife was and how "work practically comes to a halt whenever she meanders between the machines and desks." The expert was likewise enthralled to follow love stories, family and real estate disputes, and threats for lawsuits.

The matter lay dormant and would have been completely forgotten had it not been for the fact that the international security bureaucracy which—though normally sluggish—did not hesitate to send out new notifications from Helsinki and Berlin that eventually found their way to the director of the Central Bank of Lebanon. He, in turn, informed the prime minister and the minister of finance that the situation was threatening the country's prestige and its international classification as a nation with strong financial fidelity. He asked Interpol to send investigators, and so the choice landed on the one man known for solving the most complex financial crimes, including determining the identity of the "godfather" of Marseilles and southern France, and arresting him. He was the giant in the spotless white suit with the blue handkerchief sticking out of his jacket pocket, who Farid Abu Shaar watched from behind his desk, as did all the other employees, as his penetrating stare scanned everything inside Karam Brothers

Press while he headed with his entourage toward the Heidelberg XL 162, the main suspect in the counterfeit bills case. He stops to watch the process of its operation and then approaches the workers standing on it, climbs up the metal ladder to the second level and walks around it, asking the operators questions that some translate for the others. He inspects a sample of what is coming out of the machine—high-gloss color pages of a fashion magazine. The team spends a long time standing there at the end of the hall, so Farid immerses himself again in editing the text for an Arabic ad for Apple iPhone 5—the new mobile phone, its applications, the vast capacity of its memory, the high resolution of its camera. It wasn't until the inspectors had completely surrounded him that he noticed them. They entered his inner circle and closed in on him. The foreigner with a hunting dog's keen sense of smell scanned Farid's desktop and, with an unjustifiable sleight of hand snatched up the printed copy of his book, which had been placed to his left on the desk and which he never parted from, just as he never parted from the red notebook before it. Farid got up angrily, resisting this affront to him and trying to wrestle his book from the hands of this foreign investigator. The female officer rebuked him, "We have orders to take possession!"

"Take possession of what?" Farid shouted in desperation after everything that had been slung at him.

"We're searching for evidence..."

"But that's a book of poetry!"

He himself called it poetry this time, to diminish the value of his book while he watched the expert feel the surface of the pages and assess their thickness. Signs of victory appeared on the investigator's face, as if without much effort, on the very first day of his trip to Beirut and within a mere fifteen minutes of entering Karam Brothers Press, he'd found exactly what he was looking for.

The inspectors left. Persephone followed their movement from her window. Earlier, she'd been informed of the second raid by the trembling Fleur who screamed, "The police are here, Madame!" She was always wary of the police for reasons related to her expired visa and the fear of being deported back to her country. And so, the woman who lived up on the second floor watched as the black, four-wheel drive Ford Explorer slowly made its way down the narrow road toward the main street. The blond investigator seated in the passenger's seat beside the driver was holding Farid Abu Shaar's book in his hands—the woman's gift to the copyeditor and the sole bit of loot captured in the second raid.

22

The day they returned home to Gemmayze from their honeymoon in Salzburg, Persephone's mother-in-law insisted she stick the ball of leavened dough above the door before crossing the threshold. With some difficulty, Abdallah held his wife up high as he waited for one of them to find a coin—in the end it was his driver who found one at the bottom of his pocket—for her to press into the dough ball for good luck. All the while his father Lutfi grumbled about his wife and those silly customs she'd brought with her from her village to Beirut.

Abdallah was a snorer, starting their very first night. She'd get him to turn over with a little nudge, shutting off his music, but still she couldn't sleep. She lay awake, staring up at the ceiling at a shadow cast by a tree and its branches swaying in the breeze. There was something about that place that Persephone Melki didn't like anymore. She had decorated it, and everyone who saw it loved it, but she had developed a disliking for it.

She couldn't stand all the noise from the nightclubs anymore and the loud music coming from nearby streets, or the loud revving of car engines—speed demons zipping down the east side of Independence Boulevard after midnight. Then came that rumble from the new printing machine, a deep tremor that traveled through the rock walls and reached upstairs. The Quies earplugs Persephone always put in her ears before bed were of no use anymore. It felt like the whole world downstairs was constantly moving, around the clock sometimes. And the start of spring would bring the mosquitoes. Some flew near her and buzzed in her ears or even flew inside them, and others couldn't be seen with the naked eye. She'd scratch her skin so hard it would become inflamed and start bleeding. She said it was from the jacaranda trees. They attracted mosquitoes from the ends of the earth. She lit sticks of incense and mosquito repellent mats day and night. The entire house was equipped with electric bug killers that zapped every time a flying insect made contact with one of its electrified bars.

But the thing that bothered her most of all was the smell of horses.

"No, I'm not fine," she'd say to her friend in French over the phone in the morning.

"Why not?"

"That smell!"

"You told me it was gone."

"Not the smell of paint, Sarah...the smell of horses."

"What horses?"

"Haven't I ever told you we live in a stable?"

Abdallah would snort to himself, seriously doubting there were still any traces of the horses so many decades after they'd been moved to the Beqaa Valley.

"Maybe it's ink you're smelling."

Persephone would bring Fleur into it. "Don't you smell horses?"

But Fleur would contradict her with something like, "No, I smell jasmine," if it was springtime. The newcomer from her faraway island didn't know she was supposed to agree with her mistress and say she could smell that horrible animal odor nestled in the corners of the press and the house upstairs, especially on humid days. Persephone quit talking about the mosquitoes and the horses after her father-in-law Lutfi took offence at her insinuations about his mother's home and trees. She resorted to burning sticks of incense, which Abdallah, who couldn't stand the smell of them, would throw away, only to have her relight them the moment he turned his back.

She, too, started going out again once Abdallah resumed his normal routine. She accepted an invitation from her fellow graduates of the Fine Arts Academy to participate with them in an exhibit called "Beirut's Memory," with the subtitle "Identities and Fires," which was held at the huge expo hall constructed near the coast on top of the city's garbage heap.

On opening day of the exhibit, a friend of hers introduced Persephone to a stylish gentleman who was drinking champagne excessively. He traded in his empty glass for a full one every time a waiter passed by. He introduced himself as an appeals lawyer and didn't stop slicking his thick and silky golden hair back as he greeted and joked boisterously with acquaintances he found in every corner. They viewed the oil paintings together and the front pages of old newspapers that had chronicled infamous massacres. There was a charred car body with an umbrella on top in the colors of the Lebanese flag—white and vivid red. They stopped in front of what looked like a boxing ring with a confessional seat placed in the center of it. The corners were barricaded with actual sandbags, and there were plastic Kalashnikov machine guns sticking out through the spaces. There were laughing and crying theatre masks suspended from the ceiling, and projected onto the walls continuously throughout the day were scenes depicting children playing or raging battles in full swing.

The lawyer's questions were sudden and direct.

"How strange! You aren't one of those silly blondes with twenty different kinds of sunglasses!"

"How did you know?"

"You're not wearing any nail polish," he says, taking hold of her hand without asking.

He smiles and continues performing his role as tour guide. He points out some turbans clipped with wooden clothespins to a long rope in the middle of the ring.

"The white ones are generally for religious men of the Shiite sect and the black ones belong to those who can trace their bloodline back to Imam Ali Bin Abi Talib..."

He explains to her about the customary red Turkish tarbush with the white cloth wrapped around it worn by Sunni sheikhs, then moves on to the black headdress worn by Maronite priests consisting of twenty layers that no one makes anymore, and then the difference between the various headbands worn by Druze dignitaries, each according to his level of religious knowledge. The creator of the installation, which was entitled "Uncivil Wars," had the idea to bring in the clotheslines and hang abayas of every color, stoles, staves, miters, and golden-colored priest's vestments.

Then he came back to her, and asked her all of a sudden, "Why did they name you Persephone?"

"It's my grandmother's name—on my mother's side."

"Is your grandmother Greek or Italian?"

"She's from Athens."

"Does your family still fast on Tuesdays? Does your father never shave his beard to lament the fall of Constantinople?"

"I was told that about my grandfather. Only my mother is Greek Orthodox. My father is Catholic, my husband is Maronite, my paternal aunt married a Muslim man, my brother is married to a Muslim woman...We are the epitome of 'Identities and Fires'!"

"But you're not wearing a ring."

"So I don't miss out on encounters such as this!"

They both laughed. He had one more glass of champagne before stopping again in front of a wall adorned with a large painting that from a distance appeared to be one solid color. He went closer trying to decipher its charm. He pondered it a long time and then went close enough to read the signature of the artist in the bottom corner. He turned suddenly, as if he'd been stung, toward his companion who was standing back a short distance away from him.

"This is yours, Persephone?"

She nodded her head.

Her friends from the art institute had insisted that she contribute something inspired by the theme of "Identities and Fires," and so she was content with a simple canvas to which she added gradations of the color pink—just like the paint covering the walls of her house. There was also a layer of thick material she didn't paint, but instead formed scattered words on, in relief. The lawyer, when he tipped his head to the side, was able to join the letters and read some phrases out loud: "And they chanted nothing but," "Dissension," "They will be overturned," "Moderation"...

"You didn't tell me you were an artist."

"I'm not an artist."

"And you know Arabic?"

"I don't know what these words mean, but I like the way they sound."

She copied them exactly as Farid Abu Shaar had written them in his red notebook.

They continued their tour of the exhibit, reaching the "Long Memories" wing where there were lists of names of villages that had been wiped out during World War I, along with photographs of armies in their various uniforms that arrived in Beirut one after the other. And there were original documents describing the conditions of the country at the time. Some observations made by an American diplomat caught Persephone's attention. His country was still following a policy of neutrality at the time, at the beginning of the Great War, and he'd sent a handwritten letter, in English, to the Department of War in Washington:

> ...*During our passage through Beirut, bread was scarce. If there was any available, it was brown in color, or leaning toward green, bitter. Not a day goes by without seeing women and children with sunken eyes in the streets and alleys searching through the garbage for orange peels or bones, before dying of hunger on the side of the road. They dug a huge pit for them by the horse stables near the port where they buried these migrants who found their way from remote mountain villages to Beirut. Then after the war ended, they paved over it with dirt and planted trees.*

After the exhibit was over, Persephone retrieved her painting and hung it on the wall of her bedroom—across from her bed.

23

Probably the most contemptuous remark that the owner of Anwar Press made at the start of the Printers' Syndicate board meeting, was when in a very serious tone he expressed his astonishment at the Karam Brothers' nearly perfect creation.

"Pure artists!" he called them while puffing out a cloud of smoke from his morning cigar and added that one of their fake 20-euro notes cost them less than thirty cents, giving them one of the highest rates of return in the whole world! Others whispered that someone inside the press had snitched on them. It was not possible to get at the members' true sentiments after the Syndicate chief closed the subject, complaining that it was not an easy thing to shut down a press that had been in operation for a hundred years, and moved on to the other items on the meeting's agenda.

The people whose jobs were threatened by the possible closure included fourteen designers—only one of which wouldn't have to worry, because another job was waiting for her as soon as she said the word; eleven machine operators—three of whom were close to retirement age; five production technicians; three graphic designers; two calligraphers—a man and the son he apprenticed; five typographers; four binders and gilders; two photographers; two accountants; some warehouse workers and delivery men; cleaning workers; secretaries. In all there were sixty-two male employees—forty-six of whom were married, three divorced, and thirty female employees—only nine of whom were married. In other words, Lutfi was not exaggerating when during an appointment that he scheduled with the minister of the interior, who belonged to the political party the Karam family had long supported in elections, he complained that a hundred families' livelihoods were at stake. It was that lieutenant colonel in the Financial Crimes division—a Druze, he whispered—who was after them. "If it's money he wants," he said, "We'll give him money, but make him leave us alone!"

Switching to a different angle, Lutfi boasted that his family had accomplished true national unity: one could find Maronites, Orthodox, Armenians, Sunnis, and Shiites at their press. There even came a time on Abd al-Wahhab al-Engleezi Street when the Muslim employees outnumbered the Christians at the press. In the beginning, the Muslims specialized exclusively in lettering— handwritten and then typeset. The Karam family rarely hired a calligrapher who didn't hail from Basta or the Baydoun neighborhood. They became experts at engraving letters, pouring metal molds for them, setting the type, aligning the pages, and everything having to do with writing.

"You waited three centuries before consenting to the printing press, and then another century before printing the Quran!" Lutfi Karam would rebuke Master Anis al-Halwany, standing there before him, as if he were the representative of the entire Muslim world. Then he would go on to tell him how in 1600 a Maronite cleric managed to transport a printing press that he'd brought in secretly by way of Italy just to print one book with it.

Lutfi raised his finger and repeated, "One book!"

It was the book of psalms in Syriac and Karshuni[10] on facing pages. Not a single copy of it still survived. All that remained was a description of the illustration on the first page of the book:

"A cedar tree in whose shade one can see a swan, a spring, two wheat stalks, a cross and a cap..."

Master Anis didn't know how to share Lutfi Karam's astonishment at what Bishop Sarkis al-Razzi had done. In Rome, the Bishop had paid in gold, from his own pocket, the price of the machinery and title deed for the letters. Then he sailed across the sea with them and transported them on mule, back over the course of many days, all the way to Saint Anthony Monastery high up in the mountains of North Lebanon. The convoy was stopped along the way by soldiers of the Ottoman Wali of Tripoli. But after inspecting his cargo they let him pass through and continue on his way because this was the very first time— and would also be the last—that they'd ever seen such equipment. Similarly, Anis did not feel any personal guilt for Sultan Bayezid's decision in 1485, and after him Salim the first, who overthrew his father and killed all his brothers and their sons, to forbid printing in Turkish and Arabic. Neither Anis nor anyone like him who worked with setting lines and pages, and inhaled for many long years that concoction that Guttenberg himself invented in Germany in the fifteenth century, and which no one had modified in any major way since: seventy percent lead, twenty-five percent antimony, and five percent tin. They ingested trace amounts of it when, in their haste, they would hold the letters between their lips or neglect to wash their hands when they left the typesetting table for the breakfast table. They were born white, but then their fingers would turn black first of all, and over time their whole complexion would turn gray and shiny. Eventually one would die of lung cancer and another would suffer symptoms relating to lead exposure, despite the strong recommendation an English pastor with blue eyes and a long white beard made early on to the workers at the American Press, to drink a bottle of milk every day to prevent lead poisoning.

Then along came the Maronite press workers. They came down from their mountain villages and were skilled at operating the machinery and knew all the intricacies of how they worked. A standout among them was a man who came knocking on the door of Karam Brothers Press when it was located near Sagesse High School. His attire, his accent, and his thick fingers didn't seem to suit the introduction he gave himself as being an "Offset Master." He looked more like one of the end-of-summer apple pickers or a wicker basket weaver, but out of necessity they decided to try him out. He sat down at the printing machine as if he'd only just left it and began arranging the lines of text and the pages with great ease and skill, while making very few errors. They hired him at a decent wage. His coworkers soon discovered his beautiful voice and started asking him to sing *ataba mawwals*[11] to keep them entertained while they worked. Then one day when one of the workers who did bookbinding quit his job at the press, the man suggested they hire a young man from his village, an "artist," he said, at hole punching, stacking, gilding, and bookbinding. After that, he brought along another relative whose skill he praised and who truly established himself as an expert in all types of machine repair. All of them were diligent workers who did their jobs conscientiously and never missed a day's work. They flocked into Karam Brothers Press one after the other, kinsmen, a brother bringing in his brother or neighbor, an uncle recommending his nephew. They became numerous, and the scent of the village exuded from them. If they got to talking quickly with each other, it was difficult for others to understand what they were saying.

They all came from one village on one of the mountain slopes of the Keserwan District where some Mariamite nuns had inaugurated a big printing press that made prayer books in a variety of languages for distribution all around the Middle East to all the sects loyal to Rome. All the males from the village learned the printing trade as a result, and it became their sole source of income.

However, Lutfi Karam's father preferred the Muslims born and raised in the Beirut area. He said they were "easy to please" and didn't ask for too much, like the newly arrived migrants who came from their villages to take up residence in cramped apartments and came to work carrying their "lunch bags" filled with boiled eggs and cheese, to avoid wasting their wages on lunch in the nearby restaurants.

They remained strangers to the city without any friends there, but when the various fronts became embroiled in the war, many of them picked up arms and started working night into day. They would come to work at the press in the morning, directly from their guard duty behind the barricades in the shopping district at night. It was ascribed to some of them to have fended off infiltrators trying to attack at night, or to have brought down a sniper who had been taking control of the Nazareth Street neighborhood, dangerous activities they never boasted about a single day and which were hard to believe in light of their discipline and selflessness on the job.

They took pride only in the fact that one man among them, a simple blacksmith from the town of Rayfoun, declared one day the creation of the first republic in all the East, in support of the peasants and chasing out the feudal lords. On the occasion of a press-worker strike that was putting a lot of pressure on the union to end it, those tradesmen, the sons of peasants, printed a secret pamphlet and distributed it to their associates to drum up support. In it they revived the oath of the Antelias populace of 1840 in which "Druze, Christians, Alawites, and Muslims" made a pact among themselves to be of "one voice." Any Druze who betrayed the oath would have to leave the company and be divorced from his wives, and any Christian who went back on it "Would not be entitled to a Christian burial." Lutfi feared them, because they were a tight-knit network of relatives, and if they decided to halt work, they could paralyze the press any time they liked. He decided not to hire any of their new relatives flocking into Beirut, and it didn't make any difference to him that his wife had been overjoyed to hail from the village next to theirs, where she took him to visit once and could never persuade him to visit ever again.

When Lutfi Karam met Farid Abu Shaar for the first time all alone at the press, after the police raid and after Farid returned forlorn from the main headquarters of the Internal Security office, he thought he was one of them—a remnant of those press-worker villagers of bygone days; a highfalutin peasant who spoke words "bigger than his britches." People told Lutfi that during the second raid, the police snatched Farid's book from right under his nose, shared some heated words with him, and then left. Lutfi didn't seem at all surprised. With a snide grin taking shape on his face, he turned and went to look for Anis al-Halwany.

24

S ome sort of blue demon must have been dwelling inside Farid
Abu Shaar's writings. His notebook got stolen at night, then
got returned to him, also at night, remade in the most beautiful
fashion, before being snatched away by a Dutch investigator in
street clothes in broad daylight. The next day he told his mother
not to expect him home and not to worry. He was going to stay
late at the press.

Everyone left for the day. There was no one at the press except
Farid and the night watchman who came in to see if the place was
empty. Wearing sneakers, the watchman suddenly appeared, without
having made a sound. They called him Abu Ali.

"No one told me you would be working at night!"

Farid ignored him. The watchman asked him to shut the
door behind him when he left; it locked automatically. Abu Ali
lived alone in his tiny apartment near the press where he stayed
up all night in front of the television.

Farid turned his desk lamp on. The place was empty except
for the black-and-white photo of the press's founder with his
handlebar mustache, looking directly at him just like during the
day. He'd sat directly in front of that photo since day one. He
opened the phone book and picked up where he'd left off earlier,
halfway through the alphabetical listing of family names. There
were very few errors, but he insisted on checking every word
carefully while the sounds of mosquitoes buzzing at night and

electric fans whirring rose above the diminishing noise from outside. He plodded through the never-ending columns of names. When he raised his head from his work, he didn't notice anything stirring out of the ordinary. He tracked down errors until his eyes got tired and then nodded off, the red pen in his hand and his chin resting on his chest. He knew how to sleep sitting up. He often succumbed to a nap after a heavy lunch. He wasn't sure how long he'd been asleep when he was awakened by a loud ringing sound like the crash of a cymbal inside some grand cathedral. It wasn't clear if the sound had come from inside the press or had emerged from his own depths, and for a moment he thought the thing he was expecting to happen was going to happen. He sat up straight. He listened and waited, but all that reached him was the nighttime music from the neighborhood outside.

He went back to his phone book, determined to stay there until dawn. He became lost in all the Lebanese names and nodded off again. He propped his cheek on his hand and drifted off until his elbow slipped out from under the weight of his head and his face hit the desk. He winced from the pain that kept him awake long enough to get through the names beginning with the letter "*rā*'," which he managed to reach around one o'clock in the morning. He wasn't going to start a new letter. He doubted anything was going to happen. He thought about gathering up his papers and heading home. He was exhausted, and now that the pain had subsided, his last nodding off turned out to be much more elegant. His chin was firmly rested on the palm of his left hand, keeping his face nicely propped up, and the red pen was held between the thumb and index finger of his right hand, which rested gently on the pages of the phone book in front of him.

And that was how Persephone found him when, unable to sleep, she opened the kitchen door leading down to the press, after having stepped out onto the balcony and feeling a nip in the air she hadn't felt for several months. She took a few steps down the stairs in that night of insomnia and there he was: the manuscript fellow in that contemplative position, like someone jotting down images from his imagination as they came to him in succession, or as though, with eyebrows arched, he was listening to a voice speaking to him and faithfully recording every word. From where she was, he didn't appear to be sleeping because he was sitting in a normal, upright position. She tiptoed in the dark toward the circle of light encompassing him like a halo, expecting him to feel her presence at any moment. He didn't move. She got closer and saw his eyes were shut. He was asleep. She stood gazing at his lips and broad shoulders until she woke him up—her long stare woke him. He saw her and gasped, but she put her finger to her lips to quiet him, as if any words he uttered might alert the night watchman or somehow ruin their encounter.

He woke up, straightened his tie, stood up slowly, and fiddled with the button of his jacket while trying to decide if he should fasten it before coming around to the other side of his desk. He couldn't take his eyes off her, casting that look at her he was born with. He didn't blink, as though if he were to lose one second of looking at her, then the thread tying them together would be severed, they would regain consciousness, and the spell would be broken. Without looking away, he reached over to turn the desk lamp off, drowning the vast hall in total darkness. He wrapped his arms around her. She clung to him and closed her eyes. She smelled of sleep. They embraced each other in the dark for a long time, hearing nothing but the sound of their own breaths. He didn't kiss her, and she didn't kiss him. They were like two people standing in a dream that lasted until the sound of a car horn outside broke it. Farid bent down to pick her up. She resisted, but he was resolute and so she gave in to his strength. She wrapped her arms around his neck as he carried her toward the Heidelberg XL 162.

He had planned out this objective of his before, even if it was at night when he finally accomplished it. He'd begun daydreaming about it ever since meeting her in her husband's office the day he entered the press for the very first time and had never been able to stop replaying it in his mind since. He chose numerous places for their encounter—his friend Ayyoub's hotel, his house in Furn al-Shubbak, his bedroom on a day when his mother was out, and even the family house in the village, up in the mountains, despite the difficulties of this proposition. He also imagined proposing they meet there, between the machines, on a sofa he noticed had been placed back there for the machine operators to rest on after hours of standing.

A concealed private spot walled off by the giant machine— he carried her toward it while trying to control his trembling limbs, so excited was he to actually be living out his dream— the meeting of their two bodies. He embraced her. She sank into him. He wished if only the corridor between the printing machines wasn't so narrow he would dance with her, twirl her the full length of his arm, before lowering her carefully onto the couch. Like one lost in ecstasy, she lay down, welcoming him as he leaned over her, cupped her face in his strong hands, pulled her to him and began playfully kissing her neck. They were in a state of semiconsciousness, somewhere between insomnia and sleep, embracing each other with a lot of passion and a lot of tenderness. Whispers and kisses all over the place. Between one sigh and another, he lifted her nightgown and sat her on his lap. But their passionate embrace and his desire to enter her, that had been ignited by the touching of their naked bodies, remained unfulfilled.

Persephone was the one to stop everything. Suddenly, she put her hands on Farid's chest and pushed him away. Slipping from his grip, she got up and stood there as if just realizing where she was and what she was doing. She looked all around, making sure the press was empty, and put her nightgown back on. Farid sat there limply on the sofa, shocked by what had happened to them. She tiptoed over to his desk in a hurry to put her slippers on before passing by him once again, fleeing, with her hand over her mouth, half-asleep, as she said something in French about that place and its stench.

He didn't understand, as usual. He tried to speak, to ask her a question, but she took off up the stone staircase.

He gathered himself, stood up, and headed back to his desk where he remained for several minutes, reenacting how he had been sitting when she had suddenly appeared. He left the phone book open to the page he was working on and left. He closed the door to the press behind him. The air was refreshing and the dawn *adhan* was coming softly from a radio in the watchman's room. Come to find out later on, the watchman hadn't slept but had stood behind the window waiting for Farid to leave. The copyeditor-writer could hear a couple of alley cats hissing at each other. He cast a glance up to her window and set out for his mother's house on foot. He was whistling happily as dawn broke on the streets of Beirut, swimming atop a wave of bliss. He breathed in what was left of the woman's scent on his clothes and repeated their names as if chanting a spell: Farid and Persephone. He didn't like his own name—common and dull. If he got married and had a son, he would name him Adonis. Nothing was more reliable than mythology. The city was slowly waking up, and as he passed by the French College of Medicine, Farid remembered a line of *zajal* he'd memorized. He sang the opening line aloud.

> Take pleasure in me, O poetry, yes be pleased
> It was from my voice the nightingale learned to sing

He grinned at the early shift of municipality workers heading to their little jobs, or others returning with tired faces after a long night. He had decided to save his appetite until reaching his mother's kitchen, but when he got close to home he saw a little restaurant he knew at the beginning of Red Cross Street opening its doors with the dawn for the workers of the early shift. He waited for the owner to bring him a bowl of hot *foule*, which he'd fixed to Farid's liking as usual with extra olive oil and lemon. The most delicious meal to have at dawn, he dove in up to his elbows, feeding himself big pieces of pita bread, onions, and hot green peppers. His mind settled down after that, and sleep came sweetly to him with the rising heat of day.

25

When officers from the Anti-Financial Crimes division, headed by Lieutenant Colonel Hatoum, raided the press on those two consecutive occasions, it really wasn't anything new. Karam Brothers Press was used to such visits from the military. A hundred years earlier, not long after opening its doors for the first time, an officer by the name of Alexandre Ferdinand-Marie de Parsifal had swooped down on the press, unannounced, with an escort of French soldiers. Fuad Karam feared the new profession he'd set up for himself was not going to have a bright future. He secretly planned to win the colonel over by inviting him to the Tabaris cabaret nearby and introducing him to the call girls there. Once again, he regretted not having chosen to go to Alexandria…

Concerned with military secrets, the head of the "Levant Forces" pulled out documents detailing general staff, flowcharts of administrative leadership, and demographic statistics for the five nations soon to be established: one for the Alawite lands, one each in Damascus and Aleppo, one for the Druze in Hauran, in addition to the nation of Greater Lebanon—the first ruler of which summoned Fuad Karam to the fledgling government palace in order to rebuke him. The journal *Al-Ma'rad*, which was being printed by Fuad Karam's press, had published on the bottom of its front page an illustration of a barking dog, without any caption or commentary. Innuendos turned into suppositions and eventually certainties that found their way to French ears, all claiming that the drawing represented the ruler Leon Cayla himself. Cayla had not summoned Fuad to have an audience with him, but rather to threaten—in French—to close his press down and to accuse him of ingratitude.

"We should have left you under the yoke of the Turks…"

Another time, when the press was on Damascus Highway, it was raided by French mandate soldiers. They came to seize *Al-Barq* newspaper because the poet Al-Akhtal al-Saghir, its owner and sole editor, had published an elegy in honor of the King of Iraq, Faisal bin al-Husein, on the front page.

> For you, all the capital cities donned themselves in black
> All the funeral processions in the world could not shed enough tears

The King had been a friend of the British, which was ample reason for the French to consider it an affront to their prestige and worthy of reprimand.

During World War II, Monsieur Jean Helleu ordered the seizure of pamphlets calling for the release of some politicians seeking independence who were being held at the Citadel of Rashaya. He likewise ordered the censorship of newspapers and reserved the right to look at the editorial, which quite often resulted in the column reserved for it to the left of the front page of *L'Orient*, for example, being left completely blank. After the occupying forces withdrew, the new Lebanese morality police were next to come, searching for pictures of nude women that were reportedly being printed by Karam Brothers Press. Then came the "*Deuxieme Bureau*" as they called the military information service, which put its nose in everything. The specialty of the Internal Security Service was all matters relating to religion and religious sects. The director summoned the press owner, and after an introduction in which he declared that he was personally in favor of freedom to criticize, even to the point of heresy, he went on to convey a message from Christian clerics who disapproved of the press's having the audacity to print thousands of copies of the Jehovah's Witnesses' version of the Holy Bible, which was said to contain false Christian doctrines. Volunteers belonging to that group were going around to people's homes and giving away free copies, to the point where some puritanical families had started putting up signs on their front doors with a picture of the Virgin Mary and a caption that read: *Jehovah's Witnesses: Do Not Ring Bell.* On the same occasion, the director of Internal Security also conveyed hearing that the Maronite patriarch was very angry about the publication of a book of historical research in which its Protestant author presented proof that Christ lived in the southwest region of today's Saudi Arabia, using as a basis the similarity of place names appearing in the Bible, and that Jesus had had brothers and sisters, making a mockery of the doctrine of the immaculate conception. And the biggest scandal was over a book Lutfi Karam had no idea could be so dangerous. A very polite and well-mannered young man had come along asking to have his manuscript, "The Epistles of Wisdom," published at his own expense. It sent a shock wave at the time that almost landed him and the author in jail. It turned out that in the book the author had revealed for the first time ever the divine secrets of the Druze faith. Another scandal occurred after that over a book criticizing the Companions of the Prophet.

All this happened during a beautiful time that saw the emergence of nationalist hopes, up until the Arab forces were defeated in the Six Day War and Israel occupied more Arab lands, leading to the Palestinians' taking up arms of all types. They left the refugee camps and divided up into competing factions, all with similar names and all of whom wanted to print flyers with pictures of their fallen martyrs embellished with lines of poetry by Samih al-Qasim and Mahmoud Darwish. Beirut was plastered with posters against making peace with the enemy and for independence of the western Sahara and Wadi al-Dhahab and elsewhere, to liberate Eretria from the rule of Emperor Haile Selassie. A young Beiruti woman of Jewish origins made a documentary film entitled, "We Have All of Death to Sleep." It began with a song.

> The hour of liberation has chimed! Get out colonists!
> The hour of liberation has chimed, from Oman to Dhofar!

And there was a huge demonstration demanding the return of the three Emirate islands from Iranian hegemony. Pamphlets and articles were distributed announcing the determination to topple the Lebanese compradors clique beneath the blows of the united alliance of laborers and tobacco farmers and the Palestinian resistance. Accompanying this great program were the writings of Kim Il Sung that were printed and given out for free, and the sayings of Lenin about the state and revolution were discussed with the kind of reverent piety given to interpretations of the Holy Bible. And a huge number of cassette tapes were sold with Sheikh Imam singing, "O Egypt, rise up and be strong!" Meanwhile, a young poet from a poor village in South Lebanon took the stage at one of the universities, and recited to a throng of fired-up students:

> Beirut! Daughter of hard steel!
> You bank of Asian blood!
> You whore of a thousand unknown identities!

One night a truck full of explosives blew up in front of Karam Brothers Press. It was intended as a warning, followed by a phone call threatening to blow it up completely if it continued publication of a poetry collection by an Iraqi poet fleeing his country who'd come to them to have his book edited. When he came to Lutfi Karam, he was dressed in tatters, probably hadn't bathed in a month, and his poetry contained lines such as these.

> They are opening fire, alas, on Spring
> All the stolen money they amassed will melt away like ice

The reference was to the dictatorship that was coming to Iraq, God knows how. He was found a few days later, stabbed in the heart. He bled to death, but the circumstances of his murder were unknown, because the investigators couldn't find evidence of breaking in or forced entry into his shabby room near the Rawsheh neighborhood.

Civil war broke out, and ID checks became common. Two Karam Brothers Press employees who lived in West Beirut were kidnapped. Some big strings were pulled, and they were released, but after that the Muslims stopped coming to the Christian Gemmayze neighborhood. Only Master Anis stayed there at the press, even slept there, because they couldn't manage without him, until they were able to "smuggle" him to Basta to join his family. He stayed in Basta until the war came to an end. One of the warehouse workers was killed by a sniper on his way to work at the press.

They suspended all operations for a time and then resumed once they became acclimated to the war situation. The armed militias became their best customers. One of Lutfi Karam's main services was to enlarge maps pinpointing the "coordinates" of enemy targets that they wanted to shell. A member of the organization that called itself *Silah al-Ishara* (Communication Service) supervised the printing and made sure it didn't leak out. They published an Arabic language magazine written in Latin script. They would edit it dozens of times, embellishing with poems praising the "Land of the Cedars." They used the magazine to establish themselves as direct descendants of the people who gave the world the alphabet and the color purple, and whose "daughter" was kidnapped from the civilization at Tyre to establish Europe. Lutfi Karam printed pictures of their beloved martyrs for free, shaded by a drawing of a cedar tree and the saying, "He died so Lebanon could live." In return, they secured imported paper for him, duty free. One day when they were unloading a shipment from one of those ships, a heavy parcel of paper fell off the crane and landed on Lutfi's leg. He'd had to use a cane ever since.

Despite that incident, the Karam family believed it had escaped the civil war with minimal damage. That was until a missile exploded that was likely one of the last ten launched into the Beirut sky the evening the final peace accord was signed, distributing power among the various sects. The missile hit the press at night. A fire ensued, but fearing it would spread to their homes, the neighbors managed to bring it under control. By the end of the war, a total of seven printing presses had been destroyed in Beirut and its outskirts. Twelve had been looted, and a similar number were forced to shut down, because most of their machinery and equipment had gotten outdated and their owners couldn't afford to update them. A wave of newcomers entered the printing press scene, and likewise a number of warlords advanced to important political positions, forcing out the traditional leaders. "Karam Brothers Press, Est. 1908," was one of the few to survive.

26

Joop Van de Klerck didn't need much more than a microscope from the forensics lab at the Internal Security general administration office and a couple drops of purple liquid that he applied to a small clipping of paper to prove what he already knew—that he had found a perfect match of the paper they were searching for.

He submitted two copies of his report—one to the Lebanese public prosecutor and the other he emailed to Interpol and then sat in the lobby of Le Gabriel Hotel waiting for instructions from Lyon. He watched people going down the street through the window—a fat man wearing a long white robe and an Arab kufiyya walking ahead of his wife veiled in black as they entered the hotel through the revolving door. He was speaking loudly to her without looking at her. Another man, in his forties, wearing a black cowboy hat, sat buried in a leather chair with his razor thin MacBook computer on his lap. There was a kid walking a big dog that was scaring a couple of young nuns who were rushing away in the opposite direction.

Then he switched to leafing through the pages of the book Master Anis al-Halwany printed using his grandfather Abdelhamid's equipment, at the behest of Mrs. Persephone Melki. What Van de Klerck had assumed to be merely a decoration for the front cover was actually the book's title—a single drawing in the center of the first page, the word "The Book" that Farid Abu

Shaar settled on calling it in the end and drawn the way Omar al-Bazerbashi had done it on a separate sheet of paper: a triangle in which he used the *alif* (ا) as one leg, the *kāf* (ك) for another, and the *bā'* (ب) as the base. All the other elements were contained inside this tent—the *lām* (ل) and the *tā'* (ت) and the dot for the *bā'* (ب) which ended up above the horizontal line of its letter instead of below it, along with the two dots for the *tā'* (ت), all swimming inside the triangle without neglecting the *kasra* vowel for the *kāf* (ك) and the *fatha* for the *tā'* (ت) and the *sukūn* (ْ) planted in the page space.

As for the author's name, it was flowing and cursive, written in stationer style with a slight shadow effect. In order to hide any evidence of the mission he'd undertaken with such precision, Master Anis had asked al-Bazerbashi to write for him, in *Thuluth* calligraphy style, four common words inside a frame: deception, passion, Beirut, and 'the book.' Each word was on a separate sheet of paper, size A4. He also asked him to write in *Kufic* style in smaller font size a list of names of people who worked at Karam Brothers Press, included among them as camouflage, the calligrapher's own name Omar al-Bazerbashi, and his own name Anis al-Halwany, and the name of the copyeditor Farid Abu Shaar. The calligrapher was used to getting such requests from as far back as he could remember and no longer bothered to ask what they would be used for.

As he flipped the pages, Joop Van de Klerk didn't pay attention to the reading direction of the lines. He looked them over with his head heavy from the three glasses of white Lebanese wine he drank at lunch. Then he realized that the letters at the beginning of paragraphs always appeared on the right, so then he made sure to turn the pages in that direction. He paused to look at the ornamented shapes—the *'ayn* (ع) bunched up on itself, reminding one of the bowl of Hygieia with a snake twined around its stem like it appears on pharmacy signs; or the *fā'* (ف) stretched out on its back—half odalisque and half mermaid with her tail illuminated in lavender and greenery all about; and the *jīm* (ج) with its leg extended upwards and branching out like a spider web and forming some indecipherable hieroglyphic symbol.

A young woman appears in all her elegance, walking as if modeling on a runway, and casts an interested glance over at the Dutch giant with the blue eyes. He recalls everything he'd heard about the "*joie de vivre*" and other perils encompassing Beirut. He hopes his stay there will be extended, the surprises having begun the moment he stepped off the plane. He had still been in the middle of traffic in the police car that picked him up from the airport—with its siren having been turned on by the driver for no reason, when he got a text message from an unknown number—a very specific bit of information written in French: "Go to Karam Brothers Press in Achrafieh in East Beirut. There you will find an Arabic language copyeditor. Grab the book of poetry on his desk in front of him and you will find the evidence you're looking for."

Van de Klerck's phone number had been listed on the police alert informing local authorities of his arrival. He smelled something fishy about the text, and he had decided ahead of time that he would delay arresting any individuals without being absolutely certain they were guilty, or unless he got their clear confession. He asked the police woman accompanying him to assist him in the raid the next day.

The moment they entered the spacious Karam Brothers Press hall, she whispered to him in English—the reason she had been chosen to help him—that the guy with the bright red necktie to his right was the Arabic editor and that there in front of him was indeed a book. They walked toward the huge machine and then turned and closed in on him all of a sudden. The Dutch officer touched one of the pages of the book at first and then picked the whole thing up.

Joop Van de Klerck remembered well the terrified face of the copyeditor at that moment, and the way he stood up to resist as if warding off a stab to the heart, his hands straight out in front of him toward the investigator making his way out the door and his eyes shooting out flames before plopping down onto his chair in despair, not understanding what was happening to him. The way he looked and his innocent, spontaneous reaction were an indication to the investigator of some tampering with the investigation, or possibly an attempt to send him to the wrong place under false pretenses.

The yawning Dutchman resumed inspecting the book with its rare, elegant guise. Letters that intertwined and embraced each other, with ends flourishing upwards. Letters in *Thuluth* style that Abdelhamid al-Halwany had carved and cast himself in the prime of his youth after being told by Mr. Pearson when he worked at the American Press, "We brought you the printing press, now it's up to you to Arabicize it." Letters with *nunation* and completely marked with short vowels, with butterfly shapes, floating commas, and miniature letters hovering around them. Words that proceeded forward as if carried on a howdah of symbols. And as if that wasn't fancy enough, each page was girded on all four sides with a border, shrinking the usable space and giving the printed words inside it even more prominence, and leaving space in the margins to be filled with birds, heavenly harps, little angels, in addition to crowns of laurel.

Al-Halwany had given it everything he had to please Mrs. Persephone. The moment he was finished making the copy, which pleased him very much, he rushed to show it to her. She flipped through the pages with obvious delight, stealing glances at Anis as if she hadn't expected this family friend to come up with something so lovely and elegant. She looked him directly in the eye and asked if he had told her husband or her father-in-law what he'd done, to which he shook his head no. Then she asked if he'd made only one copy and he nodded yes. As a child, he and his buddies in Basta did not consider head nodding to be a definitive answer, whether yes or no, if it wasn't accompanied by words.

Anis wanted to pay tribute to the memory of his grandfather Abdelhamid. He didn't think he would ever get another opportunity, so he made use of everything his grandmother Imm Mustapha had saved in her kitchen beneath the jars of jam and pickles, embellishments intended for spaces between paragraphs, and those meant for the ends of chapters; ovals and intersecting circles, rose blossoms, and that final touch—the drawing of a naked cherub, a baby shooting an arrow from his bow seated on a throne of greenery scattered evenly left and right.

Joop Van de Klerck got up from his comfortable chair in the lobby and wandered around in the liquor store and the bookstore adjacent to the hotel outside. In the evening, the chief of the financial crimes division informed him, over a table spread with Lebanese mezze dishes, that the owners of Karam Brothers Press were highly reputable people, well-connected to those in power in the country, and that the Lebanese investigators hadn't found any evidence in the ledgers or in the computers. Van De Klerck, however, had something else on his mind.

"Who reads the correspondences between you and me? Who here has access to my phone number?" He didn't want to tell him about the strange text message.

"I don't know, but people sometimes ask for phone numbers of investigators in order to pass on private information."

The Dutchman was not convinced by the lieutenant's feigned ignorance. Obviously nervous, the chief changed the subject, telling him about a young man who worked at the same press who had come to see him at his office to inquire about a manuscript he claimed some agents from his department had confiscated. This coincidence provided one more bit of proof to Joop Van de Klerck that something fishy was going on behind his back.

"He inquired about a manuscript or a published book?" he asked.

"I remember him talking about a notebook with a red cover and handwritten pages."

The two men exchanged descriptions of the young man, most notably his arched eyebrows, confirming that they were indeed talking about the same person. They agreed to call him in for questioning together, even though Joop felt as though the financial crimes division chief was not sharing everything he knew.

27

The first time Husein al-Saadiq contacted the press was by phone, just before Abdallah's wedding. He sent a set of fine, hand-painted porcelain china as a gift when they got married. He came to the office for a visit, a silver ring with a jade stone setting around his finger and a chain with a sword pendant dangling from his neck. He started out conveying greetings to Lutfi Karam and his son from his father, their old friend. They closed the door, so no one would interrupt them. The praises went on for a long time about their long history in the printing business and how they were the "gold standard," not only in Lebanon but throughout the Arab world. They thanked him, and then he whipped out a USB drive and slapped it down onto the table.

"But your press is on the brink of bankruptcy," he said in his feeble voice. "That would be a great loss to Lebanon. Your bank debts are in the millions, and that's in U.S. dollars. Here is your solution! Al-Hajj Abu Husein has many friends, but he loves you and prefers you over all of them."

They tried to object, but he went on heedlessly. "Don't deny it. You know we have well-informed sources…"

They both knew this man, who'd never entered a school in his life, who'd spent his childhood helping in tobacco farming before emigrating as a teenager to the Ivory Coast, having been sent by means of a coincidental friendship with an officer who led the rebellion in the north. He was sent to work in the diamond trade, the route between Africa and the Amsterdam market. He had come to the Karams while vacationing in Lebanon wanting to have Imam Ali's *Nahj al-Balagha* printed in an elegant manner only Karam Brothers Press could do, so people said. He ordered three hundred copies, bound with a fancy velvet cover, to give as gifts to all his friends, customers, and relatives. He came back another time to ask for ten bound sets of *Bihar al-Anwar* by Muhammad Baqir al-Majlisi, all forty volumes in each. He was a jolly fellow, rotund and loud-spoken. They heard he was in trouble for smuggling and had established some new and effective political connections that protected him from any kind of legal prosecution.

Abdallah inserted the USB drive into his desktop computer. He showed his father the photo of the twenty-euro note, front and back.

"Take your time. Talk it over. We'll get together next week," Husein al-Saadiq said, interrupting a long silence mixed with contemplation about profits and risks. "At any rate," he added, showing the extent of his familiarity with things, "You have your own experience with such matters…"

He was alluding to something that had taken place over forty years earlier, before the young man was even born—an "experience" that lasted a few short weeks. It happened during that period when people decided to pick up arms and set up cannons, when the city was divided into two camps. They came up with the idea to flood West Beirut with counterfeit money. When war breaks out, as they said, people resort to using whatever weapons they have at their disposal. They persuaded Lutfi to imitate the blue hundred-lira note with the Cedar Forest on one side and Beiteddine Palace on the other. They imagined their enemies on the other side of the green line struggling amid a flood of worthless money hitting "their economy," causing chaos among them and thus weakening their ability to fight back. With the help of an artist, they printed a truckload of unconvincing counterfeit bills. They had no idea how or where to start trying to unload them, until they hooked up with an armed faction who took a shipment of them, in return for some antique plates and figurines they claimed were Phoenician, but turned to be worthless fakes, too. During the relatively quiet lulls in the fighting, that group was able to sprinkle some of the bills here and there, but their effectiveness was very limited, especially since their coarse texture made them very easy to detect. The vast majority of them ended up "coming home" to the eastern side they'd been generated from. Word got out and the militias seized the remaining bills from the Gemmayze press. They warned Lutfi Karam not to pursue such activities without consulting the leadership first, and that was the end of that.

Husein al-Saadiq came back, full of confidence they'd be on board with the plan. He pulled out a piece of paper from his pocket—a page torn out of a catalog with the name, specifications, and a picture of the Heidelberg XL 162 on it.

"Import this machine and we'll take care of the customs duty for you ..."

He pitched a business agreement to them, and at the end of the meeting he put forward a check for four hundred thousand U.S. dollars as his investment in the project, the remaining hefty cost of which the Karam family would have to come up with, with a detailed budget of all expenses to follow. Then Abdallah got hurt in the explosion in Beirut and everything came to a standstill waiting for his recovery and the arrival of the new printing machine. Husein returned six months later. He looked long and hard at the wounds and at Abdallah's face. He asked for a detailed account of what happened and for the reason why he was in the vicinity of the explosion at the time. He asked about the surgeries he'd undergone and was reassured by Abdallah's current medical condition. Then he got to the point.

"Who's at the press at night?"

"No one…except the watchman."

"Who is he?"

"An Iraqi."

"An Iraqi here?"

"He's an upright fellow. A Syriac Christian forced to leave the Mosul area. He has a wife and a child."

Husein was not comfortable with the night watchman's description.

"Let him go. We'll send you a man with experience, trustworthy. He's single and lives alone."

"What will we do with this other poor guy and his family?"

"We can't take any chances."

They agreed to run the machine during the day as a regular part of the press functions and once a week—Husein insisted on that without elaborating—*only once a week*, two men would come at night to run the machine without leaving the slightest trace.

"Do they know how to run the Heidelberg?" Lutfi asked.

"They were trained on it in Germany. We sent them there especially for that."

"Just us and Master Anis…" the younger Karam answered without adding any clarification, much to the surprise of those listening who were asking who from the other side would be part of the working team.

Al-Saadiq showed his dismay once again. "Who is this Master Anis?"

"Anis al-Halwany."

"Where's he from?"

"Beirut."

"Which Beirut?"

"Al-Basta."

"If we'd wanted to involve Muslims in this venture," he said, his fears confirmed, "then we would not have sought you out. At any rate, you're responsible for security, and keeping the work secret."

"Anis al-Halwany grew up here with us," he answered, reassuringly. "His father worked in our press, and his grandfather, too. We can vouch for him!"

From the very beginning, Anis proved he was of use. He got scared when he first looked at the project, but then he accepted it like someone not personally responsible who was merely taking orders from the owners of the press, just as he'd done in all sorts of matters. His eyes lit up when the subject of the right paper to print on came up.

"Let me take care of that!"

When the central bank decided to introduce new denominations of currency and print them in Lebanon, they invited bids they were unable to consider due to political pressure, threats, and the desire to divide up the bounty, forcing it to be awarded as usual up to that time to the British Thomas De La Rue Company. One of the Beirut printers that had been confident they would win the contract went ahead with purchasing tons of special paper used for printing currency and ended up with a warehouse filled with it. Anis remembered hearing that they were trying to sell it below cost. He had it transported by truck and delivered to the last cellar of the press, where he hid it inside the wall. It had been common practice for builders of arched-stone structures to put in a hidden space somewhere inside everything they built. It was mentioned in front of Anis that the press's hiding place had been used to store weapons. That was a secret shared by him and Lutfi Karam alone; even Abdallah didn't know it existed. Anis was in charge of it. Whenever the two experts came at night, he was careful to enter the last cellar by himself and retrieve only the exact amount of paper required.

Making a good copy of the digital photo was not the difficult part of printing the fake euros. The hard part was incorporating all the security features and getting both sides to be perfectly parallel, something that required lengthy and numerous attempts to improve it little by little, until finally on that conclusive night when Lutfi, Anis, and Husein spent a long time comparing the currencies in disbelief. They held their version up to the light dozens of times, checking the water mark, praising its precision, making sure the signature of the Head of the European Central Bank was there, that its fictitious sequence number was there, the map of Europe, and the magnetic strip.

All the preparations and planning were complete, and then what was called "the July War" broke out. Countless Israeli airstrikes, missiles fired in every direction, hundreds of casualties, all the bridges destroyed, hundreds of thousands fleeing their homes…As a result, government supervision grew lax and off sailed the first shipment of Finnish euros from the port of Beirut while they waited for the airport to reopen in the fall. From there, fake travelers were recruited to carry luggage to Africa, to be sent from there by sea or air to wherever it could be sold to professional distributors. The returns were dispersed at the rate of one quarter to Karam Press, one quarter to the Al-Saadiq family, and one half to the anonymous entity that took care of security on the road, transport, distribution, and turning the profits into real currency.

28

F arid's mother woke him up at noon. He wouldn't dare return to the scene of his crime. Everyone might notice the way he positioned himself behind his desk in the direction of the stone staircase, waiting in expectation for Persephone to come downstairs to the press. He wanted to talk about her, to say her name aloud. There was no chance of bringing her up with his mother who at the mention of anything to do with women would advise him to marry the girl at once, rather than playing around here and there, and so with the first signs of sunset he sped off to Los Latinos.

In the taxi, the radio broadcaster was reporting on armed battles going on near Beirut Arab University. The taxi driver was vying with the radio and speaking over the reporter's voice, complaining and bemoaning the current situation in the country. Farid wasn't able to catch anything of the news report except the sound of heavy artillery in the background, followed by the sudden breaking off of the broadcast. The driver instantly concluded that the reporter, who was standing in the midst of a battle, must have been hit by gunfire and might even have been killed. When Farid got out of the taxi, the driver was still waiting for the live broadcast from the war-torn streets to resume.

Abu Shaar entered the club and immediately asked Wasim, the bartender whose masculinity was a popular topic of gossip, to bring him a cigarette, which he lit up and savored like a newly inducted smoking connoisseur. Ayyoub came along soon enough, and Farid sat him down in front of him. He held his hands and wouldn't let him turn his attention to the club that was nearing opening time or even answer his cell phone. His eyes danced as he told Ayyoub he didn't have anyone else to tell his story to, and if he didn't tell it, he would explode.

"What happened to you?"

"A woman."

"You too?"

"I had a night like no other…"

Here was the master of precision, who sculpted his words as if someone was listening and recording every word in the eternal book of eloquence, now spewing words all over the place. Lovesickness had turned him into a chatterbox trying to recapture with words and gestures what happened to him the night before, from beginning to end. Then, as though an oral description wasn't enough and drawing the woman's enticing figure in the air with his hands fell short of the mark, he pulled out his red editing pen. Ayyoub thought his friend was going to draw his lover on paper, but with an emotional quiver in his voice, which he lowered as if he was about to reveal a big secret, Farid grabbed the menu in front of him and drew a map—the press, the road leading up to it, the jacaranda trees, the front staircase connecting the two stories of the building. He marked the spot where he believed they met up and where the event occurred that Farid Abu Shaar could only allude to with a hand gesture and an obscure, sheepish grin. He was recalling an event he feared would never repeat itself. He told Ayyoub about the darkness and the voices and the phone book and the way she suddenly appeared as if coming out of his dream, "She was alabaster…" He hesitated, noting that she resembled his lost book. This made his conversation partner laugh out loud.

He elaborated heedlessly, unbelieving. Taking in a deep breath and closing his eyes, he remembered her scent; he tasted her on his

164

lips and tongue. There was no way to describe the softness of her skin except to rub the palm of his right hand against the back of his left. But apparently all this was merely a series of introductory remarks, leading up to something he opened his hands and rolled his eyes for, naming it and bringing it back in his celebratory tone: "That delightful secret in her eyes, that invitation jumping from her face whenever our eyes happened to meet!" He was off and running, unstoppable, as if having returned from a dream beyond his wildest imagination. He called her his "set of fine crystal," his "warm bread," and said what they had between them didn't need and would never need words. He hadn't understood a thing from their brief exchange because she spoke French in a very elegant accent using words that were very difficult for him, but nonetheless she enchanted and excited him. He didn't stop until Ayyoub's burning curiosity made him interrupt.

"Well, who is she?"

"The press owner's wife."

Ayyoub whistled with surprise and let out a boisterous laugh over the quick-witted notion that came to his mind. "Next time I'll send your friend Luna to her husband and you'll be even!"

Farid told Ayyoub about the police raids and what happened to him with that tall blue-eyed man who couldn't find anything better in the whole big press with all its machinery and archives to pounce on than his book. He didn't even read it, just felt the pages, bent them and listened to the sound they made between his fingers. The police woman accompanying him nearly pointed her gun at him. His book…it slipped from his hands as if it had a secret energy of its own.

"Fair is fair," joked Ayyoub. "You lost the book and won the woman!"

Then he asked about the raids and what was going on at the press, but Farid, who was reliving the magic of his special night behind the Heidelberg Speedmaster XL 162, answered him with a line of poetry by Imru' al-Qays in which he talks about "a gazelle that ensnared my heart and fled," just as Luna happened to appear in the doorway.

She brushed Farid's cheek, petted his hair, called him "her handsome poet" and said, imitating him with her eyebrows raised and lips protruding, that she liked him better when he was frowning and serious. Her real name was Roxanna, but Ayyoub gave her the name Luna. He always gave them easy, two-syllable names. She'd come from Moldavia on a Middle East Airlines flight from Bucharest, along with ten other girls that came in one big batch. It was the largest deal Ayyoub had ever concluded during his history in the profession. They got distributed among the various clubs, and he kept four for himself, one of which was Luna. She'd had a very poor childhood. She had to walk all the way to school from her father's little farm in Moldavia that he worked all by himself. After losing his wife, he nursed his grief by driving his old tractor that puffed black smoke out of its exhaust pipe into the air like a steamboat until he couldn't take care of his four children anymore. He sold his land and spent his days shut off inside the house, drinking cheap vodka and crying for no reason. Roxanna fled to the city. She enrolled in an art institute during the day and worked in restaurants at night, until she met this slick Lebanese guy named Ayyoub. He knew how to treat the girls. He was extremely generous with them at the restaurants, spoke glibly about work opportunities in Beirut.

"You'll be your own boss," he'd say. "You'll sit and talk with the customers, they'll be drinking but you won't, and if you're a virgin now, you'll come back home to your country here still a virgin if you choose."

She wasn't a virgin. A week after arriving in the Romanian capital, she'd gone with a girlfriend to a dance party. When a group of buddies caught sight of this newly arrived country bumpkin, they winked at each other and poured her one glass after another. She didn't resist the first invitation to the upstairs bedroom where she left a drop of blood on the sheets and two tears of sorrow and joy on the pillow when she woke from her drunkenness.

In Beirut she didn't get drunk, took appointments with some, and saved her money although she still hadn't decided what she would do with it. Ayyoub became like an older brother to her. Now he took advantage of her having come over to keep Farid occupied and turned his attention to running the club as patrons started streaming in. Luna sat near "her poet," but it wasn't long before she got up to tend to two men who'd come in talking about the fighting in the city, the number of deaths, and how the casualty count in the news always starts out small and then increases little by little.

"I bet the number killed goes up to twenty!" one of them said as the other called to Luna by name. "Not to mention how many injured!"

They knew the young man she was standing beside was not a customer with the means to take care of her. Farid didn't feel jealous this time. He didn't have a right to that jealousy he felt every time he found Luna sitting with a man and he knew she'd made a date to meet him after hours, in one of the hotel rooms. That night Farid felt he couldn't possibly be unfaithful to Persephone Melki. He shut his eyes and breathed in her scent, the perfume of the princess waking from her sleep.

29

Everything between Persephone and Abdallah fizzled out right from the start, over the course of the music-filled week along the Danube that they chose as their honeymoon, and which Persephone planned out in detail with the help of a travel agency. On Monday, their first intimate night together at the Corinthia Hotel Budapest, Abdallah was a bit of a bore. He insisted on turning all the lights off and drawing the curtains. He ended up with a sore shoulder from all the tossing and turning. She regained a bit of her good mood on Tuesday with the Hungarian Symphony Orchestra's performance of a Bela Bartok sonata and Johann Strauss's "Morning Leaves Waltz" at the Budavar Castle. In the evening, Abdallah tried to make up for the night before by doubling his passion and efforts in bed. The next day he claimed to be exhausted and went straight to bed as soon as they got back from a soiree featuring the music of Dvorak at the Philharmonic Concert Hall in Bratislava. He grudgingly accompanied her on Thursday to a performance of "The Marriage of Figaro" at the Vienna Opera House and then let her go up to the room by herself when they got back to the hotel while he sat on the comfortable leather chair in the hotel lobby solving the crossword puzzle by Michel Laclos in *Le Figaro* magazine, several copies of which he'd brought along with him. When he finally showed up after midnight, he didn't try to wake her. She felt him come in but pretended she was asleep, preferring that over dealing with his antics in bed. On Sunday morning, she went by herself to hear Beethoven's "Solemn Mass." It was while she was there, looking at the faces of all those handsome men listening reverently inside Salzburg Cathedral, that she realized her marriage to Abdallah Karam was not the best thing that ever happened to her. They returned to Beirut Monday afternoon in dreadful silence.

A pang of excitement found its way into Abdallah's heart when she told him she was pregnant. He started hugging her in a fatherly way, holding her hands and patting her hair, even in front of other people. Her belly began to swell, and when the doctor told her she was expecting twins he backed off once again. Sometimes he'd claim he had a cold and didn't want her to catch it, and other times he'd complain about work and worries about the press's debts sucking up all his energy. So, she turned her back to him and occupied herself with the pregnancy for months. Then the accident occurred and placed before her the real possibility he could die, which she read all over the doctors' and nurses' faces the first couple days after it happened. She remained uneasy, even after hopes for his recovery were raised. There was Abdallah, lying in a coma, hanging onto life by a thread, until finally he began to recover and settled back at home in the guest bedroom.

The doctor said he was confident Abdallah was fully healed but asked his wife to "test him out in bed," as he put it. So, Persephone snuck into his room, the night she started having insomnia. He was snoring lightly, deep asleep. She slipped quietly into the bed and slowly got closer to him. She touched him from behind and he moved a little. When she tried to put her arms around him, he jolted up as if he'd been bitten by a snake and started shouting incomprehensible things in his sleep. He woke up and realized what was going on. He sat up in bed and turned his back to her, embarrassed by his actions.

She left the room, still a prisoner of his injuries—his bruised-up face, his open head wound, his shoulder stuffed with metal. She thought it might be embarrassment about his appearance that was keeping him away from her. He seemed content just staring at her from a distance. She saw him in the mirror. Whenever they were alone together in the house she'd catch a glimpse of him in one of the mirrors she'd put up everywhere. He'd glance at her furtively, giving her strange looks that were something between nosiness and desire. It was as if he didn't know her, as if she didn't know him. As if he were surprised she was there. He'd find her sitting combing her hair, half-naked, and come up behind her by chance, or on purpose. She became convinced he was opening her bedroom door every day. He'd open it just a crack before going down to his office in the morning and watch her lying there fast asleep. After that he installed security cameras at the press and insisted on putting one in the living room, to catch any robbery attempts or anything else, so he said. Persephone would drape a black cloth over the camera and Abdallah would remove it. She'd come out of her room with bare shoulders in her flimsy nightgown and wouldn't know whether she should look directly into the camera or ignore it.

She felt sorry for Abdallah, who she surmised was desirous but impotent, and smiled when her mother-in-law hinted that they needed "a little boy" in the family. She couldn't see any way out. She introduced her daughters to music and cartoons. Two black circles started to form around her eyes, which she covered up with morning cold cream. Night was a battle for her. She was sleepless and complained about the odors and the mosquitoes, without anyone to commiserate with. She spent her long hours of free time reading her crime novels. She got good at solving them and quickly grasped the clues pointing to the criminal. She stayed stuck this way until a chink opened up in the wall.

That all started the day the young man with the red notebook came into Abdallah's office, and she asked to speak to Abdallah at the club and they said he wasn't there. It was a simple sequence she followed repeatedly. She'd ask Abdallah where he was planning to go after work at the press, then she'd phone that place shortly after and find out he wasn't there. She started enjoying trying to catch him, excited by the idea that he was lying, hoping with all her might to catch him in the act. As Abdallah's health improved, his schedule changed. The rhythm of his day changed. He stayed out late in the evening, left work in the middle of the day. She coaxed Sabine and Nicole into saying they wanted to talk to him, and when she'd try to reach him on his cell phone, she'd find it turned off. Then what really opened her eyes was his appearance. She noticed the smell of perfume on him—the same man who in a temporary lapse in shyness declared to her once that he preferred the body in its natural state. She recognized the scent—*Fahrenheit* by Christian Dior. When he left his cell phone on an end table in the living room one time, she picked it up and took a quick look. A smile formed on her face at the sight of women's names stored in the memory—Nanette, Frida, and strange addresses, like "Golden Shore" and "Los Latinos," text messages that looked like they were written in code, about obscure rendezvous. Her suspicions were confirmed when he came back in a big hurry to get his phone.

On her part, she also regained her appetite. She resumed her Thursday luncheons at the Bouillabaisse, reviving friendships with women she hadn't seen in a long time. When she discovered for sure that Abdallah was seeing other women, she knew he was really healed. She was delighted at this discovery. She didn't want him to be impotent. She was freed from his prison, the prison of pitying him.

After her tumultuous night down at the press, Persephone awakened to the sound of Nicole whining that Sabine had stolen her hair ribbon. Fleur was tending to her, but Persephone curled her knees up to her chest and went back to sleep until noon. When she awoke and sat up in bed, as was her custom, taking in a deep breath to make sure the smell of the night had gone, she noticed her right hand was stained, as if she'd dipped it in an inkwell. She must have picked up the stain in the darkness of the night before between the inky printing machines. Black blotches of it were smeared on her pillow, too. Standing in the mirror to wash her hands, she also discovered two little blue spots on her neck—bite marks from the passionate nighttime encounter. She shrugged her shoulders nonchalantly, took a shower, and spent an entire hour carefully painting her fingernails and toenails. She tried putting a black scarf around her neck, carefully tying it in a way to hide the marks. It also matched nicely with the delicate red linen dress with the open back that she hadn't found the strength to put on before that day. She wore it for her own sake and sat on her usual sofa reading the graphic novel *Fog Over Tolbiac Bridge*, smoking with enjoyment and resting her elbow on the balcony's guard rail. Her phone didn't ring, and she didn't call anyone.

They had lunch together. Dudul had wine, which was unusual for him at noon. Persephone devoured a plate of Fleur's favorite dish—Caribbean style seafood. Then, claiming she was hot, she removed the scarf from around her neck, not caring if the two blue marks showed. All Abdallah said was that her dress was pretty, and he hadn't seen it before. She told him it was the first time she put it on; she'd bought it on their honeymoon. After lunch, she went back to her bedroom. When she looked in the mirror, she was pleased at the way her face looked. It was clear and rested and the marks on her neck from the night before were gone. She decided to do what she had neglected doing up to that day: surrender herself into the hands of a beautician, apply facial masks to nourish her skin, eat right, exercise, and do all those things.

30

Despite the first police raid, the work didn't stop, especially after word spread later that afternoon that the police had visited other presses in Beirut, meaning they weren't singling out Karam Brothers. The two Heidelberg specialists sent by the al-Saadiqs continued to show up at eleven o'clock every Thursday night, greeted by Master Anis. They came wearing sneakers, too, never smiled, each carrying a backpack containing everything they needed. They worked in silence, diligently, and if they needed to consult each other about something, they spoke softly. Anis didn't know either of their names, owing to their strict economy of words. They never asked him a single personal question.

As soon as they arrived, he would go get the paper for them from its hidden location while they went right to work programming the machine to spit out sheet after sheet of euros, printed front and back, for hours. Then all that was left to do was to cut them, stack and bundle them, erase the program from the machine's memory, and reset the counting meters back to where they'd found them so none of the workers who came the next day would notice the Heidelberg had been operated at night.

At dawn, they would load the cash—fifty one-hundred-thousand-euro bundles—into the small truck parked outside the door, near where the night watchman kept vigil. They'd exchange good-bye hugs with him, calling him "Brother Wajih." That was their only show of emotion through the duration of their late-night shift before taking off to deliver their cargo into other hands that knew how to send it on its way. No trace of the nighttime operation was left at the press, and no trace of the money was left in Lebanon.

Abdallah, in turn, didn't stop either. He seemed caught in some sort of whirlwind of his own. He'd become obsessed with wine and collected as many bottles of Château Lafite Rothschild as he could, all vintages. He negotiated the purchase of two purebred Arabian mares from their British owner, in an attempt to revive his grandmother's legacy. He tried to buy his wife's silence on her birthday by giving her a ring from Chopard's with a diamond said to be extracted from ancient mines in India and a dazzling red ruby in the shape of a heart from Mogok Valley, all mounted on a rose gold setting. He bought a Porsche Panamera Turbo S that he drove home at dawn like a maniac, with his chauffeur seated beside him, from Casino du Liban, the place his love of gambling had brought him to.

He started out playing the slot machines, then advanced to the blackjack table, before finally making his way over to Classic Roulette. Intoxicated with people's constant praise for his gambling genius, he tried to play the odds. He stuck with the same table, and the way he distributed his bets drew the attention of the other players, but no sooner would he get close to a winning combination than the management would change the croupier. All his calculations would fall apart, and he'd have to start all over again.

☙

In his frenzy, Abdallah was trying to race the clock, before the inevitable occurred—an ending that wasn't long in coming, as things started getting serious with the second police raid and the arrival of the international investigator. Many at the press hadn't noticed the book that the investigator nabbed off of Abu Shaar's desk and neither did they understand the significance of that sudden visit. But the al-Saadiqs got the message: no matter how much they stayed in the shadows and looked after every detail, they knew that Interpol and Europol were intent on getting to the bottom of things and dismantling the network; the Central Bank of Lebanon had been informed of the situation, and the authorities could not play around with the country's financial reputation. Husein al-Saadiq would not reveal his sources, but he wasn't going to risk making a mistake.

"Nothing lasts forever," he said, with the wisdom of the ancients, and then added, "They didn't find anything on us. We got out without any casualties. We will stop the nighttime printing, and we'll also stop using the fake company names that have been giving us cover—since they're no longer of any use. And we'll wait to see what develops."

In other words, Abu Husein would move on to other affairs—trafficking diamonds or weapons. Nothing stemming back to the al-Saadiqs would be left at the press except for the night watchman who would continue to stay vigilant, keeping his ears and eyes open until things at the press returned to normal. In fact, he completed his mission by informing Husein al-Saadiq of what he'd witnessed going on at night in the press. Husein, in turn, called Lutfi Karam to give him the details.

Lutfi was also of the mind that there was some sort of internal breach going on, and he didn't trust his son's wife. He sat in his leather chair, pounding his cane against the floor of the office nervously as he waited for a female employee who'd been in there a long time to come out of Abdallah's office.

"Did you tell your wife what we've been doing here?" he blurted.

Abdallah answered negatively and reminded him it was the third time he'd asked him that question.

"Fine," said Lutfi, raising his voice. "How does she know we meet up at night with a man whose voice sounds like a woman?

Does she go down to the press at night? Have you been leaving that damn door between upstairs and the press unlocked all this time?"

Lutfi's voice grew louder and louder. Abdallah stammered an answer. His father quieted down when a nicely dressed man came in carrying a file. The man pulled out some papers, handed them to Abdallah, and Lutfi asked what they were.

"Contract renewal for the insurance policy on the Heidelberg machine and on the press and the house. It's with Mediterranean Insurance Company, the one Perso's brother Salim owns."

He said it as if responding to his father's accusations.

After the insurance agent left, Lutfi asked Abdallah if he could read the insurance policy. He delved into all the details and asked for a copy he could take with him before resuming his series of questions.

"What was your wife shouting about after the police came the first time?"

"She wanted to know why they were raiding us. She's gotten very nervous in recent days."

"Is that why she smashed the snow globe and I ended up stepping on all the broken glass?"

After a brief silence, Lutfi cast his stone.

"Why don't you get a divorce? I know a talented lawyer good with these kinds of religious court cases who tells me annulments are possible now for Maronites."

Abdallah's face was filled with shock at his father's suggestion.

"Get a divorce? What for? I love my wife!"

He denied what people said about him being at odds with Persephone.

"If you're getting along so well, why don't you try to have a son?" he asked, pointing to the picture of his grandfather, the founder of the press, at the front of the hall, with his thin moustache and cowboy hat. Lutfi hadn't yet been granted a grandson who could carry his name.

Lutfi got to the "heart" of the matter.

"There's someone who's not supposed to be at the press at night who stayed working all alone until dawn…"

"The copyeditor? He asked my permission to work late to finish proofreading the telephone book."

"The fellow with the arched eyebrows?"

"Yes."

"Who hired him, you?"

"We needed a copyeditor and he came along at the right time."

"I don't like him. I found him here after the first raid. He was alone at the press then, too, and said he'd been to the Internal Security headquarters claiming to have lost a manuscript that was very valuable to him. And now he's spending the night at the press?"

The thing Lutfi Karam had come to tell his son remained lodged in his throat. He couldn't find a good enough lead-in for it. As he got up to leave, he asked, "He stayed here to proofread?"

"That's what he told me."

"Take a look at the security video from last night. Find out exactly what he was doing."

"Why?"

"Abu Ali, the night watchman, said he didn't like his behavior… Check the nighttime recordings," he repeated. "Check the cameras. Don't forget."

That was the best Lutfi could do to tip his son off. In his heart, he heaped curses on that copyeditor he believed hailed from the same village as those Maronite workers they'd gotten rid of.

On his way out, he concluded his visit by posing a question to himself. *How did we end up with this guy here?* Then he added, *Whatever the case, he's going to pay!*

31

Farid started having doubts about his family early on. At eighteen, he went with one of his churchyard buddies to visit the boy's grandmother in a dark, lower floor room. She'd give his friend money on Sunday mornings if he let her smother him with kisses. She asked the boy about Farid—what was his name, his father's name, his grandfather's name—until, after running through the names of all the villagers and repeating these names to herself, she arrived at what she'd been looking for.

"Ah...You're *jalab*!?" she said, in a tone somewhere between a question and an accusation.

He didn't understand what she meant right away, but he felt insulted. This expression continued to haunt him whenever he heard the family being praised or if, for example, he was asked how he was related to so-and-so of the Abu Shaar family and Farid would suffice it to say that there were many people with that name scattered throughout God's vast universe. It all came back to him again at his father's funeral as he sat in the front row beside his two brothers on that cold day and they listened to the priest struggle in his sermon to link this modest barber from Furn al-Shubbak to the glorious deeds of his family members around the country and abroad.

Farid went back to his original doubts. He opened *Taj al-ʿArous* dictionary and read the following:

"*Jalab*: that which is *juliba*—pulled along—such as horses, camels, sheep, or household goods, or prisoners." Then he checked in *Lisan al-ʿArab* and even *Mukhtar al-Sihhah*, and it became clear to him—the image of a herd, a herd of goats, with some other strays or animals purchased by other shepherds following them down the road. Those strays could be his grandfather and father. He interrogated his mother. She rattled off her answers in a sharp, high tone that was unlike her usual calm composure. She repudiated all the rumors and lies, and spilled out stories to him he'd never heard before. An old uncle who owned half of the land in the village married two women. His two wives died before his time came, so he didn't have an heir to inherit his fortune, and it ended up going to his relatives who became embroiled in a dispute that lasted a long time. Some tried to prevent "your great-grandfather" from getting his share by making up stories about him, and by protesting his name being registered with the Abu Shaar family's civil registry during the time of the French census. After a long battle, "our house" in the village was all he got, and the land around it. Farid knew his father Halim and his grandfather Said a little bit. Said used to sit him on his lap out on the balcony of the village house. He'd crack walnuts for him, peel them with his thick fingers, and predict Farid would turn out to be a genius. He asked his mother about this great-grandfather of his, what his name was, but she said she didn't know, ending the conversation with an appeal to stop sticking their noses into all this "ancient history."

He quieted down about his roots until his modern Lebanese history professor at the university told him he'd come across a handwritten biography of the Abu Shaar family. With a letter of recommendation in hand, Farid headed to the Institute of Oriental Literatures where he was greeted in whispers by a Jesuit monk who led him down to the basement. They crossed through a space that used to house the old Jesuit press. Farid asked if they still kept the old machines somewhere, and he told him that he studied the subject very closely and was certain, based on some correspondences, that the Turks raided the press and sent it to Damascus. He said he had come across the diary of a Syrian monk who wrote on a single page that the Catholic Press was said to have been moved to Damascus, but it never happened. "We waited for it, but it never arrived." The Jesuit father of the Oriental Institute doubted the press ever left Beirut. Previous workers there told him they saw some of the machinery in use at another Beirut press and that the monks were not very concerned with finding it since they'd received donations from the city of Lyon for the purchase of a new printing press.

He sat Farid down at a table and placed before him the Abu Shaar family manuscript. The writing was tiny. Farid spent two full days flipping through its pages very carefully, searching for the lost name. But to his great surprise, he never found anywhere in the family tree the name of his grandfather Said, from whom Farid might trace the name of his great-grandfather. Tucked inside the book he found the family lineage drawn on a double-sided sheet of paper that was folded in half. It was in the form of a plentiful tree, all of the leaves labeled with the names of only the men. Down near the base of its ancient trunk rooted in Yemen, the names were purely Arabic—Qaadan, Jahjaah, Qays. Then they became Biblical—Yusuf, Ibrahim, Mousa, Ayyoub—and then taken from local saints from the mountain villages of Lebanon—Arsanios, Toubia, and Zakhia, and finally ending up with current popular names like Ramy, Shaady, and even Joe and Dave.

He was very disappointed and wished with all his heart for the manuscript to never see the light of day in the form of a published book. Nonetheless, he went on reading through the family annals, about Manuel—one of the sons of the family— who was elected mayor of the city of Sao Paolo, and another young relative who won a sports medal in the 1950s, and finally reaching a section near the end of the manuscript the author said he had written down on a separate sheet and would finish adding to the book once he found a way to have it published. He also stressed that all the details had been taken verbatim from the biographer's father, who told him everything and asked him to keep it secret. However, for the sake of historical accuracy and an honest rendering of the truth, as well as a testimony to the treacherous times the people of Mount Lebanon lived through—the hunger and the torture—during the Great War, he decided to write the story down, in a compositional style that made it easy to read. At any rate, he did not mention any names in his story and made the characters anonymous. There was enough in that introduction to pique Farid's curiosity, so much so he read it and copied it down in his own handwriting into one of his notebooks.

❧

The story was that at sunset on a golden October day, a woman came along, her bones protruding from emaciation. She was dragging behind her a barefoot boy in colorless tatters with eyes popping out of their sockets. They were coming from a small village in the province of Mount Lebanon. The woman decided to head east in search of food after hearing that the blockade on the Beqaa Valley was less severe. It seems the mother and child had survived because of the miracle they found on a mountain slope—an apple tree bearing fruit in late autumn. They sustained themselves on those tiny sour fruits until they made it to the highest house on the western side of the town. The residents of the house fed them, clothed them, and took them in, out of pity and mercy. But the woman's stay there didn't last long. Two days later, the lady of the house found her gasping for breath and clinging to her son's hand. She died, as if having handed over her treasure into safe hands, she could finally rest.

It appeared that her hosts, who were of high culture and character, didn't ask more than the woman's and her son's first names. So as not to embarrass her, they didn't ask about her family or the place she came from. She left this life, leaving behind a four-year-old son who barely knew how to say a few incomprehensible words. With time and nurturing, the boy regained his health. He mixed in with the other children of the house and went to school with them in Zahle where they registered him under the name of his new family: Abu Shaar.

Months after the end of the war and the deployment of the French army in the Beqaa, a man on mule-back passed through the village, preceded by the aroma of the spices he was selling. He stopped in the square, in the shade of the old oak tree, and waited as customers began to flock to him. He asked them about a woman and child who passed through the town during the famine. He didn't reveal his relationship or kinship to them for fear of having to assume responsibility for this burden, but the family who had taken them in had fallen in love with the boy and didn't want to give him up. In fact, they let him have their own family name.

The important thing was that the spice seller told the people of the town that the village the woman hailed from had been completely deserted. None of the few surviving former inhabitants ever returned to it. Then he elaborated on the woman's story, saying she and her husband had agreed to each wander off in a different direction. She took the boy and headed east while her husband took their other son and young daughter and headed to Beirut. They wandered through the streets begging for food, but they weren't able to hold out and ended up dying of starvation. They were buried along with many other beggars. A huge pit was dug for them in a spot near the horse stables, and they were thrown into it the way they'd been found on the side of the road—unwashed and unshrouded—just like that, on top of each other.

The man on the mule continued on his way and left the town, never to be seen or heard of again, and never having explained what his connection to the family was or to that village the famine had destroyed. As for the boy, he grew up in the warm surroundings of the family that took him in. His name was added to the list of family names along with their other sons. He married, was blessed with one son, and inherited a house to live in, while his origins, and the name of his mother and his family name, remained unknown.

Farid Abu Shaar felt he'd learned everything he could know, or ever want to know, about his past.

32

After everyone left the press, Abdallah locked himself inside his office and began reviewing the security tape from the previous few days. He knew he had a long night ahead of him there in the dark amid the flashes of light flickering on the video screen. He forwarded the tape until he reached a part where the Arabic editor's lamp was on and emitting a circle of light around his desk. There he was, as promised, hunched over a thick stack of page proofs. He forwarded the tape some more, fast-forwarded— the night was long and there wasn't much to see in the footage except the editor's back turned to the camera as he sat at his desk, nothing moving except the pen he was holding in his right hand. Abdallah was at a loss as to how he was going to watch it all. He'd found the part with the copyeditor, but he didn't know what else he was looking for.

Husein al-Saadiq was the one who insisted on installing the complete, round-the-clock security system. They put one camera at the entrance, with a view of the road leading up to the press from the street of restaurants and nightclubs below, though that one required installing additional lighting for nighttime. Another camera was pointed at the jacaranda garden where nothing worth mentioning ever happened, but they thought it would be good to have one there in case anyone tried to sneak in and rob the place. One camera was installed in the back cellar in Master Anis's absence, and when he found out about it he immediately dropped a hint in Abdallah's ear giving good reasons against having it there; a technician was called in shortly afterward to take it down. One camera covered the new Heidelberg machine and the area around it, and two were scattered in the main hall between the other machines and the employees. There was one at the entryway inside the house, attached to the naked statue of Venus, that tracked Fleur's movements when she went in and out to shop. And one final camera was installed in the living room, its star being the Maltese Bichon sleeping on the sofa, or Sabine and Nicole sprawled out on the floor fighting over crayons when their mother wasn't sitting on the sofa trying to read.

They agreed to turn the system off completely on Thursday nights when al-Saadiq's specialists came to run the Heidelberg, just in case the tapes fell into the wrong hands. That calculation turned out to be a good precaution, because when the investigators raided the first time, they took all the recordings as evidence. They put an agent in the Anti-Financial Crimes division in charge of checking the footage. He watched the film very closely and carefully at the outset, but soon he realized just how daunting a task it was— thousands of hours of footage. So, he started watching only random clips, once he realized he was looking for a particular event— the printing of counterfeit euros, maybe. He didn't know. In any case, even if it was actually happening right there on the screen in front of him, how was he going to know? The way it appeared in the cameras, the machines ran routinely and the employees running them went about their assigned jobs day after day. And the copy machines were too far from the cameras to be able to make out what they were printing. He wrote up a report along these lines and avoided mentioning the fact that he hadn't viewed all of the footage, simultaneously clearing the Karam Press of suspicion.

When the cameras were first put in, Abdallah got a kick out of watching everything that went on around him—people coming in, people chitchatting, women. He could see who was headed toward his office and prepare himself, or he'd ask why the pizza deliverer came to the house twice in a row and they'd tell him that both girls insisted on having a whole pizza to herself, so he had to come back. The game exhausted its purpose. As time went on, the press employees realized the cameras were recording them around the clock. The woman with the literary quotes complained the camera was pointed at her directly and she couldn't concentrate on her work. Everyone's behavior became restrained. If anything happened to fall onto the floor, or if a heated argument broke out, there was always someone who looked up at the camera as if to see the reaction of whoever was sitting behind it. They started watching what they did and said, because many of them were sure there were microphones picking up sound to go with the picture.

At first, he tried to review what the system recorded in his absence, but he found it to be an impossible task and stopped even looking at the screen in front of him, which could be divided into squares when desired, broadcasting the angles of all the cameras all at once. If an employee he called in to go over some matter or other happened to steal a glance at the screen, she would discover that the camera filming what was going on in the living room of his house filled the screen completely.

The security cameras had lost their luster, but here he was now, drawn back to them by his father, watching the editor putting his pen to use every now and then on the papers in front of him and then returning it to its idle position. His head would start leaning forward and his shoulder would stop moving, as if he'd fallen asleep sitting up. Abdallah fast-forwarded the monotonous film until a new person suddenly appeared on the scene. It was Perso. She crossed into the circle of light holding her slippers in her hands. That woke Abdallah up. He made sure again he was alone in his office. Heart pounding, he covered his mouth with his hand and pressed the pause button with his index finger. He let it go forward a little, but then backed it up, not wanting to miss anything.

She seemed confident in her actions. She came downstairs at night to meet him, possibly based on some prior agreement. Maybe he'd arranged it with her before asking permission to stay late at the press. She stands in front of him. He's completely motionless. She peers at him and smiles. He moves, as if he's woken up. She pushes the pile of files aside, causing some of the papers to fall to the floor. She tugs the pages of the telephone book away from him in a joking manner, as if to say editing time was over. Abu Shaar gets up from his chair and comes around his desk toward her. She's looking into his eyes, captivated. Then suddenly the screen goes dark. Abdallah rewinds the recording. He can't understand what happened to the light. It was still possible with what little visibility remained to follow what was transpiring between them, like watching a scene in a shadow play. Two bodies touching one another, their shadows refracted in fragments on the book binding machine and paper cutter and along the stone wall, finally diminishing as the screen returned to its original nighttime darkness. He kept going, panting as he fast-forwarded the recording, but the blackness continued to pervade everything until dawn's first light crept into the press. One final fast-forward and it was daytime again, and the employees began streaming in for their morning shift.

Abdallah Karam's response was swift.

He copied the few minutes in which Persephone appeared and approached the desk of the man seated there who doesn't turn around to let Abdallah see his face. He saved the clip to his USB drive that contained other private documents—medical records from his numerous surgeries, the results of his periodic lab tests, receipts from weekly financial transactions he received from the "Al-Saadiq Metal Company" in the Ivory Coast the previous two years, pictures of his two daughters Nicole and Sabine in different stages of their childhood up through learning to ride bicycles, a picture of a legitimate twenty-euro bill and one of the bills produced by the Heidelberg machine, high-definition digital photos of men and women from his family going back to the turn of the twentieth century and of the oil paintings and sculptures he owned and had in his house, and a coded list of all the girls that he paid to sleep with, along with a performance rating for each one in a language no one understood except him.

He erased all the recordings he had from the eight cameras, and he decided to ask the electrician to come in the next day to dismantle the entire security system and toss the cameras in the storage warehouse. He would talk to his father about this copyeditor. He'd be sorry to see him go because, as everyone would agree, he did an excellent job and never gave cause for even the slightest disciplinary action. He'd start looking right away for a replacement. He might have already found someone—a university student who had come to see him a few days earlier, saying he'd completed his Arabic Language certificate with honors and would like to offer his services. He didn't like him, though, because he kept blinking his eyes the whole time and prattled on incessantly. And he added without being asked that, unlike others, he wasn't ignorant about computers, as if alluding to Farid Abu Shaar himself. Abdallah might have to make use of this guy after all. He'd jotted his number down in his datebook.

He put the USB back in its hiding place and stretched his suspenders with his thumbs. Perso appeared to him again, the way he'd seen her at lunch, for the first time in a long time, sexy in her red dress and black scarf, the way he liked women to be.

He took a shower in the evening and put on some light cologne. He listened at the door until she entered her room and waited for her to fall asleep. He went out to the living room wearing his pajamas, opened her door a crack, and when she didn't move, he went in and headed toward the bed. He was on fire, his heart beating much faster than normal, as if it were his first foray into the world of women.

33

Farid Abu Shaar returned to work the next day. He glanced up at Persephone's window, but when he passed by Abdallah's office he didn't stop or turn his head. He was not afraid of confrontation. He was ready to suffer whatever consequences were coming his way. He expected there to be an argument and lots of accusations he wouldn't know how to respond to. Everyone would hear the shouting, and all his secret shameful deeds would be exposed in a huge scandal. He felt his days at that place were numbered. On her chalkboard, the woman had written a quote without naming the author: "Love is like a hunt from on high." She turned to look at him when he came in, which made him think she knew what had happened and was trying to get a good look at him. He also anticipated a run-in with the old man with the cane who had his nose in every little thing.

What he didn't expect was for two officers from Internal Security to come over to him while he sat at his desk proofreading *Beirut by Night*, the magazine he'd gotten behind on during his absence. He was in the midst of editing stories with titles like, "Jackie's Face Ruined in Failed Plastic Surgery Fiasco—She'll Never Sing Again," and "A Fight between the Wife and the Mistress Breaks Out in Fancy Restaurant." He was in the midst of that when two policemen interrupted him and asked him to come with them down to the station. When he asked why, one of them pulled out a warrant for a "Farid Halim Abu Shaar, born 1980..."

"That's you, isn't it?"

"...to come down to Internal Security headquarters for questioning."

He couldn't think of anything he'd done wrong besides his nighttime encounter with Persephone. The two officers feigned ignorance of the charges against him and kept absolutely silent the whole way to the station, even amid the slow traffic.

Down at the station, he was met with two men he already knew: Lieutenant Colonel Hatoum, head of the division, and the tall foreign investigator. He answered Joop Van de Klerck's questions in English to the best of his ability.

"Do you know why we brought you in?"

"No."

Farid appeared truthful.

"What is this?"

"That's my book. Are you finished with it now?" he asked with a pang of sorrow in his voice.

"No, not yet," said the Dutchman derisively before pulling out a twenty-euro note, which he placed on top of the book and then slid in Farid's direction.

"Check it yourself!"

Farid thought this was some new trick being played on him. He picked up the book and checked to see if all the pages were the same as before, but De Klerck grabbed the book and the twenty-euro note and explained the situation plainly and clearly.

"Listen. There are serious suspicions surrounding a number of presses in Beirut concerning the production of counterfeit European Union currency—the new edition twenty-euro note to be precise—and pushing it via a distribution network into Africa, Latin America, and finally to a Central Asian country as we have come to learn, and even into Afghanistan. All the presses with such advanced printing capability have been raided, but no evidence turned up until we happened to stumble upon this book of yours."

"We became more interested in you," the Lebanese lieutenant interjected, "after you came here asking about your notebook. Don't you remember?"

Someone had grabbed hold of Farid Abu Shaar's life and started fiddling with it without asking permission, as if it were public property. And it all started the moment he'd stepped foot inside Karam Brothers Press on that auspicious day as the sun was setting between the minarets of the Grand Blue Mosque.

"What do my book and notebook have to do with counterfeit euros? I know nothing about printing. I ended up at the press by pure coincidence. And anyway, I'm just the Arabic language copyeditor..."

"Yes, but your book is printed on thermal paper model TP 250, 120-gram weight, composed of one-quarter linen, three-quarters cotton, conforming to ISO standards for weight and durability: it can be handled and folded thousands of times before starting to show wear."

Farid had noticed his book was printed on thick paper not usually used for books.

"Don't you understand?" the Dutchman said sharply, pushing at him once again the Finnish twenty-euro banknote that traveled the world, only to find its way back to Beirut in his wallet. "It's the exact same paper as the euro. There are methods nowadays to analyze the composition with great accuracy."

Farid felt the bill and with his other hand reached toward his book there in front of Joop Van de Klerck to compare the texture of the euro with the pages of his book. Then he looked into the face of the investigator like someone descending in an elevator looking out the glass window at the people standing on one of the floors the elevator doesn't stop on.

When he naively believed they'd brought him in to question him about what went on between him and the press owner's wife, he was ready to put up a fight and ready to pay the price. He had planned to say something about consenting adults being free to do as they pleased with their lives and quote some excerpts from the Song of Solomon about women and love, but instead he found himself the subject of a dry interrogation and an onslaught of questions whose answers the lieutenant noted in his log book.

"Where did you print your book?"

"I didn't print it."

"Do you have other copies of it?"

"No. I only have this one copy and you took it."

"Who printed it?"

"I don't know. I found it one day on my desk."

The two men exchanged glances.

"Where'd they get the text from?"

"They stole my manuscript at night. I forgot it on my desk, between my other papers."

"Do you think it was printed at Karam Brothers?"

"I don't know."

"Have you ever come across this type of lettering and these typographic embellishments at the press?"

"My job is to proofread everything before it goes to press. I've never come across anything like this *Thuluth* script. It hasn't been used for printing books in ages. It is the most beautiful of Arabic scripts and the most difficult to write and to print."

"You're trying to mislead the investigation, making up stories for us…"

The Lebanese lieutenant had been harsh in his judgement, causing Farid to get upset.

"I'm not misleading anyone. I'll tell you my story from the beginning. I graduated from the university with a degree in Arabic language and literature and I have a manuscript that cost me many days and sleepless nights that all the publishers rejected as if they'd signed some sort of agreement between them. I went to nearly twenty different presses. Not a single one even bothered to crack open a page and read one line of it, until I arrived at this press. I found the address in the Publishers and Printers Guide because the owners have an old permit for publishing, as well. That owner also rejected my manuscript like the others, but I somehow ended up as a copyeditor over there, and every day I feel like everyone is winking behind my back. They think I'm a dimwit. But I don't care what they think of me anyway. They're all a bunch of trivial employees. True they work in publishing, but they're not worthy of it. They deal with it in terms of quantity, weight, money. They trace their roots falsely to a country that at one time introduced the alphabet to the world. They pollute language, but I render a service to them because they couldn't have found a better editor than me. They saw me holding onto my notebook, never letting go of it, because it's a part of me. So, they waited for me to forget it, so they could steal it and make fun of me. But then I found it again a short time later, magically printed in the most beautiful fashion, there on my desk. Someone is looking out for me thanks to all my mother's prayers…"

"But where are the other copies?"

"I only got the one copy, and then you came and took it away a few days later. Even up until I got here I was thinking some hidden hand was after my papers because of what was written in them."

"What is written in them?" De Klerck interrupted. "No one here has granted me the pleasure of knowing what's in that book.

"I hope you don't say anything in there about making counterfeit money," he added cheerfully.

Abu Shaar's answer was more vague. "That book wore me out until I finally finished it. I don't know what is in it."

"You, either?"

Farid waved his hands in more than one direction. "I can't find the best way to summarize it. Not in English or in Arabic. I think my hand was writing and a voice not my own was dictating to me. Every time I read it I found something new, as if that voice would come back and add extra things. Maybe my book will continue to expand its meanings while you have it in custody..."

The Lieutenant Colonel and the Investigator were exchanging looks whose meaning was quite clear while Abu Shaar went off, unbridled, on his tangent.

"...it's filled with the spirit of those who wrote before me. Abu Hayyan al-Tawhidi, Abd al-Qadir al-Jilani—"Bazullah al-Ashhab" (God's Grey Falcon), St. Ephrem the Syrian—"the Canary of the Holy Spirit," and many others, but at the same time, my book is my own and does not resemble anyone but me."

Lieutenant Colonel Hatoum interrupted to ask him if he had anything that could help the investigation besides these far-fetched fairy tales of his. When he didn't get any answer he said, "You'll be charged with concealing information and misleading the investigation."

"Will I get my book back?"

"Unfortunately, no," the Dutch investigator replied. "It's hard evidence and will travel with me tomorrow on the plane to Amsterdam, and from there to Lyon, France. I know a translator of Arab origin, maybe she's Lebanese, who is called upon by L'Elysee whenever the French president receives an Arab leader who doesn't speak French. I'm going to ask her to read some passages from your book for me."

Lieutenant Colonel Hatoum then expressed his feeling that this young man was totally innocent, and that maybe someone was trying to frame him for something.

As for Farid Abu Shaar, he figured the matter would be concluded with a few more words and that would be it, until the Lieutenant Colonel called over two officers and asked them to take him to the holding area of the Internal Security main headquarters to wait for his case to be decided by the investigating judge.

34

On a bitterly cold morning in the fall of 1918, inside a train car stopped in a clearing in the middle of the forest some sixty miles outside Paris, nine men—three officers from the British navy, two French generals, two German politicians, along with a general and a navy officer—signed the armistice that would end a war that lasted four years. At 10:59 p.m., just one minute before the battles were scheduled to end, American Major Henry Gunther became the last soldier to die in combat. It was said he was killed by friendly fire, after failing to stop when commanded at an Allied Forces checkpoint. He was drunk, celebrating in his own way the end of one of the worst slaughters in human history.

Two months prior to that, Fuad Karam didn't sleep the night he snuck behind the Turkish soldiers inside Saint Joseph Monastery. He'd been overpowered by an idea that enthralled as well as scared him, and which he turned over and over again in his mind until morning. The French were coming any minute, or so the officers on Arwad Island told the owner of *Al-Wifaq* newspaper. He'd rented a boat and loaded it up with what he thought the officers needed most of all—call girls, and off he sailed. The English were on their way to Damascus, the Turks were going to withdraw and had already started packing up their belongings. In the morning, Fuad went out to the press across from his house. The door was wide open. He went inside and saw that the huge machine had been taken apart and all the books boxed up. He tried to find the man who'd accompanied the soldiers but couldn't find him anywhere that night. He made his way to Wadi Abu Jamil, the only Hebrew press in Beirut. He asked Mizrahi, the owner, about a man from the al-Halwany family who worked at the Catholic Press. After all, it was a close-knit profession and al-Halwany was very skilled.

"How couldn't I know him? I taught him Hebrew. He's the one who chiseled the characters used on this printing press, and poured the molds, and helped me operate the machines."

The short-statured Mizrahi raised his hand as high as he could, his way of describing al-Halwany. Fuad understood the gesture, which was consistent with the man he'd seen with the soldiers.

On his way to the man's house in Basta, he ran into al-Halwany. He introduced himself, gave his address, and told him how he was able to locate him. Then he got to the heart of the matter.

"The Turks are leaving. Let's get to the printing press before them!"

Abdelhamid al-Halwany held onto his tarbush, which nearly fell off his head from the surprise. "How did you know?"

"I live across from the monastery. I saw you at night and heard you."

"I don't want to be sent on *Safarbarlik*[12]. I'll die on the way."

He refused at first. He was afraid, but Fuad convinced him it was only a matter of days. "The Jesuits will reward us when they come back."

Abdelhamid al-Halwany himself was not really convinced by the reward idea. He knew the monks well. But that time when a Turkish officer slapped him in front of his neighbors in Basta still left a sting in his heart. He decided to hide until things settled down.

The very same day, Fuad Karam hired ten off-duty porters from down at the seaport and made an appointment for them to meet at night. He led them down narrow, winding roads so if they tried to find their way back there in daylight, they would have difficulty. It was a peaceful night, and they worked in silence. They worked in teams of two and even four, not knowing what they were carrying in the darkness of the night. Before the sun came up, they managed to clean out the place completely. They loaded everything up, and Fuad guided them to his brother's house which was nearby and the key to which his brother had left in his care before leaving for Alexandria. They piled everything inside the house and in the yard out back, out of view of passersby and the neighbors.

The next morning, he sent his wife and son to her family. One bit of gossip from the porters, or al-Halwany, or some nosy witness who happened to be there that night, would be enough to toss him down the abyss. Two days passed, and nothing happened, but the third evening he was filled with fear when he heard the sound of horse hooves and saw from his window a band of soldiers with carts. They searched inside the monastery and came out quarreling in Turkish. Fuad clung to the wall of his bedroom, waiting out the longest five minutes of his life. Finally, he heard their voices and wheels going off into the distance. His deliverance was complete two days later when the Turkish garrison withdrew from Beirut.

On the 6th of October 1918, the French arrived at the port, victorious. Vice Admiral Georges Varney, along with his military staff, attempted to approach amid the crowd of welcomers, but they were forced to return to their battleships on account of all the commotion. The next day, the soldiers descended to the shore, and the Jesuits came onto land immediately following them. They leapt from the battleship and rushed to check on their possessions. Father Chancel wrote a letter to the general president of the Jesuit Order saying, "We recovered most everything we left for safekeeping with nearby God-fearing Christian families. The buildings are in good shape for the most part, but as for the things the Turkish soldiers got their hands on, they've all been destroyed or plundered, like the French Medical School and the Catholic Press, which totally vanished after being loaded onto a train to Damascus."

While the people of Beirut thronged into the streets, waving the tricolored French flag, to welcome the African regiment of sharpshooters and the "Syrian Legion" coming from Haifa, Abdelhamid al-Halwany went to look for Fuad Karam. When they met over hookahs at Al-Bahri Restaurant, it was not to explore the idea of getting a reward from the Jesuits, but rather to make an honor pact together.

They swore secrecy, even from their wives, relatives, and friends. And they agreed to buy a small defunct press that had closed down during the war to use as a veil. That was al-Halwany's task. Fuad Karam bore the responsibility for the machines and the rest of the furnishings and would attest, if there was an investigation, that Abdelhamid al-Halwany did not participate, and was not even there.

Al-Halwany would operate the machines, which he knew like the back of his hand, and they would divide up the income equally. That part of the agreement was amended shortly afterward when al-Halwany realized that dividing income also meant dividing expenses, too, and profits were slow in coming, so he preferred to take a monthly salary he could get by on.

The last thing they had to do was wait. And so, they waited.

The last Ottoman Wali of Beirut, Ismail Haqqi Bey, turned over what authority he had left to the Beirut municipality council president, Omar al-Daouk. Life returned to St. Joseph Monastery, and Father Lambert, the Belgian priest with the bent back, went back to reading on the church steps in the mornings as if nothing had ever happened. He told Fuad he had volunteered for the army, but they refused him because of his deformity. Many monks fell in battle, and he always dreamed of returning to Beirut. Fuad continued to seek him out until their talk finally turned to the press. Lambert told him that some neighbors saw Turkish soldiers come at night with porters and horse carts. They transported the press to the train station, and from there to Damascus. Fuad Karam corroborated the story and added some details he said he saw from the window of his house across from the monastery. Father Lambert didn't show as much disappointment over the loss of the machines, the foundry, and the metal letters, as he did about the loss of some valuable and rare books—Sir Richard Burton's ten-volume English translation of *A Thousand and One Nights*, a nine-volume dual-language Arabic and French edition of Masoudi's *Muruj al-Dhahab* (Meadows of Gold), and numerous others. Fuad was careful not to ask too many questions so as not to raise the Belgian Jesuit's suspicions and in turn made an effort to memorize the titles of the books Father Lambert was sorry to have lost before hurrying off to his brother's house to make sure they were there and then hide them and hide any mention of them from al-Halwany.

They waited for the Jesuits to return to their monastery in the Bab Touma neighborhood of Damascus, after Prince Faysal Ibn al-Sharif Housein was expelled from there by General Gouraud. When they got there, the monks asked the owners of the press about it and were sent by the Mandate authorities to the man in charge of the train station where the shipment was supposed to have crossed, but he denied receiving any printing press in the Damascus station, adding that it was forbidden for him to inspect military shipments. The only possible assumption was that it continued on to Turkey. And so, the monks began searching for investors to help them purchase new machines.

Fuad Karam and Abdelhamid al-Halwany began their work secretly at first. Al-Halwany would bring in the orders and fulfill them in the storage units that they rented to house the printing press down by Tabaris Casino. Fuad was terrified any time an officer or employee from the mandate administration came to see him, until Father Lambert moved to Egypt and Fuad knew there was no longer anyone left from the original staff of Jesuit monks from before the war, except one old priest who could no longer remember what happened.

At that point, Fuad Karam put up the sign that his descendants still moved with them from place to place and hung over their door: Karam Brothers Press, Est. 1908. It was written on a brass plaque that was repolished whenever the years turned it black. He'd added his brother, who was off living a nice life in Alexandria without much being heard from him, out of a sense of loyalty. And he'd added ten years to the age of the press merely to suggest the family had been in the profession much longer than some envious tongues might want to admit.

35

With her interior design homework tucked under her arm, Persephone would head to the old-style building in Zuqaq al-Blat where Noubar practiced his dance performances and allowed her to be the only audience member to see his rehearsals before he performed on stage. She called him "my whirling dervish." He'd dress in outfits he made himself and empty out all the furniture from the room, leaving only a valuable Persian carpet hanging on the wall. He'd step barefoot into the center of the room and let himself get swept away by the music of Umm Kulthum, forgetting Persephone was sitting there on the floor drawing on her papers. She'd stay out late, waiting for him to tire from his choreographic improvisations and sit down beside her, dripping with sweat, his heart pounding out of his chest. He'd put his head on her shoulder and she'd lean toward him as he put his arm around her and say politely and apologetically, "Perso, I don't like women."

Noubar died before reaching thirty. He either threw himself or his friend pushed him off the building from a tremendous height. Either way, he died of love—from loving his friend too much or his friend being overly attached to him. She went to the place where he was laid out in his coffin, in a hall attached to the Armenian Catholic Church. She didn't see any priest there praying over him, and she didn't speak to any relatives or friends who were there, who were so few you could count them on your fingers. She'd never asked him once who in the world his parents were. She mourned him all alone, and he transformed into one of her legends.

So, when this man with the lofty look in his eye and the book under his arm suddenly appeared at the press, she imagined he had the kind of life that suited her. He'd be a cross between a strict man of religion and a sex maniac, a golden mouth whose words enchanted her but remained incomprehensible to her. She couldn't remember his name. She'd read it on the first page of his manuscript, but when she tried to recall it later, she failed. They said his name aloud in earshot, but it didn't stick in her mind. Ever since their night together in the press, he no longer appeared in the morning with the others arriving for work. She'd stroll between the desks in the press hall during the day but wouldn't see him. Some other guy tapping keys on a computer in front of him was sitting in his place, looking around curiously at the place and its occupants. Out of the blue, Abdallah told her the police had taken the former copyeditor into custody on counterfeiting charges. That scene suddenly reappeared to her—when she went down to the press at night the first time—when she saw Anis, Lutfi, and the young man with the strange voice holding the papers up to the light and shaking their heads in agreement.

The same Abdallah who had been so worried about the press's decline and having to let a big portion of the employees go, being late with payroll, and the ever-increasing unpaid bank debts. The same Abdallah who'd felt there was nothing on the horizon that could stop the total ruin of his establishment and its descent into the abyss, who'd always looked for an opportunity to tell his wife that this copyeditor lived with his mother and how before coming to the press he used to tutor kids who were flunking out of school. He made a point to mention that his father was a *barber* on the outskirts of *Furn al-Shubbak*, saying the names of the profession and the location with disdain. And he added that the things he wrote, which he brought to the press to be published, were plagiarized from relatives of his known for their literary genius.

Persephone couldn't understand why her husband was so insistent on telling her all these details. She asked Anis how the young man ended up in jail.

"I'm just a slave who takes orders at this press," he'd say, casting blame off of himself. "Ask Khawaja Lutfi about it."

She imagined him standing before the court, reading from his book with his hair all disheveled. Sometimes in her free time she would draw some words of his that she'd copied down into a list in her sketchbook. She'd play with the shape of their lines without asking what they meant.

The lawyer with the thick hair didn't forget her. She didn't know how he got her phone number when he sent her an anonymous message in the form of a question.

"What's the best gift you could ever dream of getting?"

"Who's asking?"

"Tour guide from 'Beirut's Memory' expo."

"You must be rich. I dream of a sculpture by Giacometti, *The Walking Man*."

In another message, she wrote to him being intentionally ambiguous, "Gogol is dead!"

"He's nothing but a 'dead soul,' anyhow," he replied jokingly. "But who is this Gogol?"

Fleur found the Maltese bichon lying under the naked Venus statue with a mixture of vomit and blood coming out of his mouth. She shrieked, and Persephone came running, thanking God that Nicole and Sabine weren't at home. She'd tell them the dog got lost and didn't find his way home. They'd imagine him living a new life in some other family's home on their comfortable sofas, which would soften the blow.

Early in the morning, Persephone resumed her intermittent texting exercises with the lawyer, out on a balcony overlooking the sea. After the poisoning incident with the dog, she needed to get some fresh air away from Beirut, and also to escape the deteriorating situation at the press.

The family took a weekend getaway at that mountain hotel that displayed photos of famous people who'd stayed there over the years—the Comte de Martel, high commissioner for the Levant, the great singer Asmahan, Agatha Christie standing at the entrance, or President Camille Chamoun, with his wife and two children. The girls were skating between the tables under Fleur's watchful eyes, while their mother read *Farewell, My Lovely*, while sipping coffee and texting on her phone.

"All the hours are cruel, but this luminous morning is bringing me back to life."

Before she receives an answer, Abdallah gets up from his breakfast in the dining hall and rushes out to the balcony, his cell phone in his other hand with the caller still on the line.

"The press is on fire!" he gasps.

He looks off into the distance, distraught, toward Beirut, as if trying to see the smoke from so far away with his own eyes. When Fleur hears the news, she lets out a scream that draws the attention of the other hotel guests.

❧

The al-Saadiq family had all disappeared. There was no one left at the press except the night watchman, Abu Ali, who repeatedly told the official Lebanese investigators, as well as the ones commissioned by the two insurance and reinsurance companies, that he had no idea how the place suddenly went up in flames and that it was the neighbors' shouting that woke him up. One of them said he saw him fleeing down the hill even before the smoke started to rise. It was said that, as usual, there had been a short circuit in the electrical wires of the Heidelberg machine, which, as the judiciary expert's report confirmed, stemmed from a dip in power that occurred when the electrical supply automatically switched from the press's private generator to public power, which came on every day at 6:00 a.m. The fire trucks had a difficult time getting to the press because of the narrow road leading up to it, which allowed the fire to spread and consume the modern machine. The majority of it was reduced to a heap of charcoal and scrap metal. The fire also reached the paper supply in the main hall and raged through everything in its path— leather furniture, machines, wooden desks—finally making its way to the manager's office where it also wiped out everything inside it. The flames licked at the door at the top of the stone stairs, leading to the kitchen. A sudden breeze fanned the flames, setting the curtains ablaze, the beds, the upholstery, the wardrobe closets, Persephone's clothes and her books. The naked Venus statue at the entrance was charred. None of the decorations and mirrors in the living room were spared except for the peacock, or at most the head of the peacock that looked on at the scene with a shocked eye while half his multicolored plumage burned. It wasn't possible to know more about the cause, because Abdallah had asked the repairman to remove all the security cameras, leaving no recorded evidence of what happened that night.

The next morning, the employees arriving for work were shocked to see the extent of the damage as the firefighters were still trying to get the remaining flames under control. Lutfi Karam stood beside the jacaranda trees, which had been reduced to blackened stumps. He thumped his cane against the ground in the face of the fire burning down his mother's house and the press he'd inherited from his father and grandfather.

Dudul and Perso extended their stay at the mountain hotel until they could find a new house in Beirut.

At a meeting of the Press Owners' Syndicate, before there was a quorum to start discussing the items on the session's agenda, the owner of Al-Anwar Press began asking "innocent" questions he already knew the answers to about the fire at Karam Brothers.

"Is the Press insured?"

"Yes."

"What's the value of the insurance policy?"

"Seven million dollars."

"Who's it insured with?"

"Mediterranean Insurance Company, covered by Lloyd's of London."

"Who owns that?"

"George Melki's son, Salim."

"Salim Melki is Abdallah's brother-in-law, right?" he asks, knowing quite well the answer to his own question. He concludes by asking, while rolling the cigar between his fingers, "They'll get the maximum payout from the insurance company. Quite a profitable affair! Didn't I tell you things in the mirror might not be as they appear?"

36

When he entered his jail cell down at the Internal Security general administration building, Farid found two silent men inside. One was there for forging the signature of a relative of his, an expatriate living in Venezuela, and selling his house out from under him while he was away. The other had been arrested at Beirut airport, for having one million Captagon pills in his possession and refusing to divulge the names of his accomplices.

Farid spent the first day lying on his back, looking up at the ceiling and contemplating what happened to him. The next day the other two gave him a brief rundown of their stories, and when a new young man was brought into the cell, he didn't waste any time doing the same. He told them how he fired his pistol at some policemen. They'd come to stop him from finishing building his house, because he didn't have a permit.

Next came Farid's turn. He smiled, propped his back against the wall, and said that everything that had happened was on account of a woman. A woman so dazzlingly beautiful that artists were rendered incapable of painting her onto a canvas. Her mother raised her and her sister in secret, away from curious eyes, in a house out in the fields. The other prisoners were expecting to hear about a kidnapping or honor crime as it sometimes happens in some parts of Lebanon, before Farid continued, saying that spring came along, and all its flowers, too, and just as the girl was picking a bouquet of narcissus, the earth cracked open and out came a carriage pulled by eight blue horses the color of the dark night sky. The Captagon smuggler whistled in disbelief and gave the other two a look, but Farid paid no heed. He continued on, saying that her sister hastened to intervene, so she wouldn't be snatched away by Hades, the Lord of Hell. That's when everyone disappeared, as if by the strike of a magical staff.

Her sister wept so much she transformed into a water spring. The guy who'd fired at the police thought about making a derisive comment, but he stopped himself from saying it aloud for fear Farid would stop talking, and the detainees had started surrendering to his story. Her mother wandered off after her, leaving the earth without fruit, and people started to go hungry. And so, the gods intervened to bring her daughter back to her. Hades agreed against his will to send her up to earth, and her sister's tears stopped flowing. But one of the orchard guards had caught the girl picking a pomegranate and saw her eat seven of its seeds. *Whoever eats from the fruits of hell can never leave.* The greatest of the gods intervened and ruled that the girl would spend six months in hell and six months on earth.

And that's how the year came to be divided into seasons.

"And what is this girl's name?" asked the guy who forged his relative's signature.

"Persephone."

"Do you know her?"

"No one knows her like I do."

"And what about you? What did you do to end up in jail?"

"They claimed I counterfeited the Finnish twenty-euro bill."

The pleasantries started to turn serious. His cellmates began asking him for more stories, to kill time…

❧

Farid's older brother hired a lawyer for him at his own expense—one of his in-laws. He told him that Farid was innocent, lived

214

in the clouds, and never in his life made enough money to even open his own bank account. The lawyer met with Farid and discovered he was not entirely aware of what was happening to him. He warned him that if he continued saying that he was under some sort of curse because of his writings and that the accusations against him were merely an excuse to steal his book, then he would not be able to help him. If they proved the charges against him, he could be sentenced to three years in jail, or even up to five years if the judge thought he was mocking the court with such claims.

The lawyer insisted on knowing how Farid's book had been printed and who printed it. He suspected he might be trying to cover for someone there, so he told him the press burned down leaving nothing much behind. It went up in flames at night when there were no employees around and the owners were away on vacation. He tried to make it clear to Farid that he wanted to get him out of the mess he was in and that "those others" had gotten off clean from counterfeiting charges after the press burned down and no evidence was left. Actually, they would get a nice profit if they got the insurance compensation, plus they'd be able to let their employees go without having to pay the legally required indemnity, since they lost their means of operation in the fire.

"You're going to be let go without any compensation, fine. But why should you get locked up in jail? None of them came to see you. They didn't ask about you. If anyone has committed a crime, it's them!"

The lawyer argued his client's innocence before the judge, but he did not succeed in getting him released. Despite the judge's feeling that the defendant standing before him was not capable of counterfeiting money and selling it, he was forced to sentence him to three years.

In prison, Farid found a copy of the Quran, which he borrowed and read standing up. He read the entire time he was in jail. He requested a list of books from his brothers, which he read while standing up, but he no longer wrote anymore. His standing and reading like that roused his buddies' curiosity in the beginning, but then they got used to Farid and developed a liking, even a love, for him.

✿

When he got out, his mother celebrated the occasion with a feast of grilled meats, tripe, plates of hummus, labneh, and pickles. She invited his two brothers to join them. They questioned him, but he firmly denied knowing anything and changed the subject to how they were doing, how were their families. When his mother went to the kitchen to get more plates of food, he took advantage of her absence to raise his glass of arak and clink glasses with his brothers.

They were in the midst of sipping their drinks when Farid suddenly asked, "Would the son of Halim Abu Shaar snitch on a woman?"

His brothers looked at him in disbelief.

"…and such a beautiful one, too, like you've never seen?"

The next day, his mother came into his bedroom holding his notebook—his manuscript, with its faded red cover. Farid was thrilled. He flipped through it joyfully checking that it was all there.

"Some man with blackened fingers knocked at the door this morning, saying he cares for you and knows you from the press. He gave me this notebook of yours and told me you were innocent, but that you shouldn't mess with important men's women…I asked his name, but he said you'd know who he was."

Master Anis al-Halwany, who could afford to be generous now—the only one who'd taken advantage of the flood of money into the press to improve his circumstances. He'd purchased a fancy apartment for his family in the Zarif quarter and freed himself of paying rent. When he'd arrived at the press the morning of the fire, he was stunned by what he saw—everything was charred and destroyed. He stood beside Lutfi Karam until he got the chance to go into the back cellar. His hiding place was intact and hadn't been touched by the fire. He knew he would be retiring from the profession, so he decided to take back his grandfather Abdelhamid's typeface blocks. He loaded them into a taxi, the same way he'd gotten himself there, and took them to his house, along with the red notebook. After a good amount of time passed and he heard that Farid Abu Shaar had gotten out of jail, he found his way to Farid's house on Red Cross Street and gave the notebook to his mother.

After lunch was over and his brothers left, Farid stretched out on the sofa in front of the television, hugging his notebook tightly to his chest. He was determined this time to never ever part with it again. The ghost of Persephone in the dark at the press came back to him, mixed with the fire that was said to have consumed the press with the flames of hell, then the owner of the horse-drawn carriage appeared, bringing the beautiful girl…and Farid drifted off into a deep sleep he hadn't enjoyed in a very long time.

❧

Early in the evening, he headed for Los Latinos. When the owner, Ayyoub, came down from his hotel room to the bar as he usually did at around 11:00 p.m., the place was practically empty. The only sound was Umm Kulthum singing "Al-Hubb Kida" (That's How Love Is) in the background. On the big screen TV, whose sound was muted, there were scenes showing unidentifiable prisoners all wearing the same orange uniform, crouching on their knees before a group of combatants, each holding a gun to a prisoner's head. It was possible for anyone watching to easily notice the extent to which the faces of the prisoners resembled those of their murderers. Ayyoub looked away from the TV screen and saw his friend Farid Abu Shaar sitting at the bar. Farid raised his hand and then lowered it. He leaned back in his chair and pointed to nowhere. He was in the midst of an intense moment, swept away by what he was reading aloud from his red notebook for Luna to hear while gently touching her bare shoulder and the base of her neck with his fingers and the palm of his hand. He read each passage through to its end with total abandon and finished each one off with a swig of Jack Daniels before starting anew. It was a very strange scene in Ayyoub's eyes, who'd never seen anyone from his village let loose with such abandon.

What caught his attention even more than that was Luna, who was forbidden from drinking alcohol with the customers and was required to empty out the customers' drinks under supervision before getting them another. There was Luna, sipping Jack Daniels, looking blissfully into the eyes of Farid Abu Shaar, as if she understood, as if she was drinking in every word he was reciting to her in his eloquent classical Arabic.

Endnotes

1   The *Muʿallaqāt* are a collection of seven or ten long pre-Islamic poems, ranging in length from 48 to 106 lines. They are sometimes referred to as The Suspended Odes, or The Hanging Poems, since they were hung at the Kaʿba in Mecca. The *Muʿallaqa* of Zuhayr Bin Abi Sulma is one of these famous poems, 62 lines in length.

2   *Mawwāl* is a traditional, melismatic style of vocal music popular throughout the Arab world, which involves singing a syllable of text while moving between several notes.

3   A *zajjāl* is a singer/composer of *zajal*—sung oral poetry. Historically, zajjāls would develop their skills in their own villages and eventually travel through other villages, sometimes inviting local village poets to a dare/poetry competition of several back-and-forth improvised verses showcasing their talent and wit, while villagers gathered around, listening and cheering on their favorite. Zajjāls would also be called upon to commemorate social occasions such as weddings, births, and funerals.

       Still a rich and active tradition today, zajjāls cultivate their reputations over the years and are highly respected and valued in Lebanese society. People memorize and repeat their favorite lines and rally in support of their favorite poets and *jawqas* (teams of poets) the way fans rally behind their favorite sports teams worldwide. This is still a vibrant, living tradition in Lebanon, though nowadays rather than travelling through mountain villages, zajal events are held at fancy restaurants where the audience can enjoy eating and drinking, while listening and watching the poets duel it out in sung, quasi-improvised verse, sometimes going on for more than five hours. Zajjāls—or now more appropriately called zajal poets—perform regularly, especially in summer, in Lebanon and around the world in Lebanese immigrant communities in the U.S., South America, Australia, etc. Some earn a sizeable income from their performances, but the vast majority do it on the side while holding full-time jobs. In 2014, Lebanese Zajal was inscribed on the UNESCO Representative List of the Intangible Cultural Heritage of Humanity.

4 The *Maqāmāt of al-Hamadhāni* is an Arabic collection of episodic stories, characterized by an alternation of rhymed prose (sajᶜ) and poetry. Al-Hamadhāni was a medieval Arabo-Persian man of letters born in Hamadhan, Iran, 969 AD.

5 The 28 letters of the Arabic alphabet may be divided into two groups of 14 consonants, the "Sun" letters (*Ḥurūf shamsiyya*) and "Moon" letters (*Ḥurūf qamariyya*). A typesetter might organize movable type according to the sun and moon letters to make it easier to add the diacritical symbol *shadda* (ّ) whenever the definite article prefix al- (الـ) is attached to words beginning with sun letters.

6 *Khawāja* is a title that became prevalent in the Middle East during the Ottoman period, used as a term of respect for notables, and eventually for Europeans, Westerners, and especially Christian Arabs.

7 Al-Imam Ali and Al-Sayyida Zeinab are holy figures highly revered by Shiite Muslims. Othman and Omar were the second and third Caliphs of Islam and are highly revered by Sunni Muslims; al-Husein was grandson of the Prophet Muhammad, and is a Shiite holy figure.

8 Charles Corm (1894–1963) was a Lebanese writer, billionaire industrialist and philanthropist, and nationalist movement leader. Georges Schehadé was a Lebanese poet and playwright who wrote in French. His play *Histoire de Vasco* earned international acclaim and was translated into 25 languages. Marguerite Yourcenar, acclaimed French novelist and essayist, was the first woman elected to French Academy.

9 Attributed to eighth-century Sufi sage Abū Sulaymān al-Dārānī, said as he burned his books, one by one, in a bread oven.

10 Karshuni is Arabic written in Syriac characters, especially as used in the Maronite liturgical ritual.

11 ᶜAtāba mawwāls are a musical form in which traditional folk poetry is sung to familiar tunes.

12 *Safarbarlik* refers to the conscription practice of the Ottoman government. Once it was announced, young men would be sent to the war front.